Return of the Selkies

Ava Le Fey

HOLLYHOCK

Return of the Selkies, Fairy Blood, Book 1

Visit me at www.avalefey.com

First Edition, 2025

Digital ISBN: 978-0-9925278-4-6

Paperback ISBN: 978-0-9925278-5-3

Large Print Paperback ISBN: 978-0-9925278-7-7

Hardcover ISBN: 978-0-9925278-6-0

Published in Australia

Dedication

To everyone who longs for freedom

And to all those who seek their true powers.

Acknowledgement of Country

This story was written on the lands of the Wadawurrung people. I pay respect to Elders, past and present, and to the Stolen Generations who also make this Country their home.

Magical battles are more fun with fae friends

Life is getting weird for sixty-two-year-old Merilea MacRury. Did the Hot Flash Hustle unleash magical talents – or is her toxic workplace making her nuts?

When a whale stranding awakens uncanny gifts, she vows to find her truth. She heads to the misty Scottish Outer Hebrides to meet her fairy ancestor Isobel.

In a wild magical romp, Meri befriends riotous selkies and dreamy dryads. When Isobel disappears and danger strikes, Meri rallies her madcap fae mob – but will she master her dazzling new powers in time to save them all?

A humorous, mid-life magical adventure with a scream of danger, a glitter of new powers, and found fae friends.

Book 1 in my new fantasy series *Fairy Blood.*

Contents

CHAPTER ONE

Who is the real me? And how do I get out of here?

For her sixty second birthday, Merilea MacRury got magic powers. She'd considered it upside down and around and around, and there was simply no other conclusion.

This morning, for example, all the tree faces smiled at her. Big round barky eyes, surprised eyebrows, knotty noses, lopsided grins. She gazed at them uneasily, then shot a few wobbly smiles back.

And she'd spotted that uncanny kookaburra a few trees ago. The bird flew from branch to branch, ever closer, staring at her with its beady, intelligent black eyes. It opened its kingfisher beak and gave a loud, echoing hahahahahahaaahooo...

She gave it a wave. *Go ahead and laugh. I know my day will be filled with horrors.*

Meri was walking the creek path, trying to boost her courage before work. Oh look – there in that shaft of early sunlight – a ghostly woman stood within a tall, pale-trunked Eucalypt, clad in lovely flowing draperies, as beautiful and remote as a Venus in a shell. Meri stepped closer, breath stuck in her throat, eyes stretched wide.

"Do hurry up," the creature said, voice soft and weary. Then the sunlight shifted, and the vision vanished. There was only mottled white and grey bark.

Meri blinked, her tingling wonder mashed with alarm.

The Hormonal Hoopla. That's when it started, she thought, tapping her pen on her nose. The Hot Flash Hustle had roared in and scorched and sweated her for a decade, then blasted out again. Phoenix-like, she'd risen reborn from the fire and floods, powered with diamond focus, simmering with energy, and lit with lightning-bright ideas.

And something more.

Magic. The notion glimmered in her mind, jiggling with heart and star emojis. It sang in her skin and called her to dance gleefully in the moonlight. Her cells knew it, even if her brain baulked: the world hummed and glowed, brimful of miracles and charms.

Here though? All enchantment surely had fled screaming to the hills. Meri glumly surveyed the open plan office, jammed with desktop computers, florescent lighting, and millennials oozing ambition and mortgage stress.

A rustle rippled through the huge space. Everyone stopped their morning chats, picked up pens and began tap-tapping on keyboards. The new manager minced through the office in her blue high heels and stiff blonde curls, cup of coffee in hand, a sadistic gleam lighting her cold gaze as she selected her morning victim.

Uh oh. Big mistake. Meri had accidentally made eye contact.

"Good morning, Merilea." The woman gave a thin-lipped sneer. "I want you to complete three media releases, a ministerial speech, and a background on four VIPs, as well arrange a ministerial event, by ten am, please." She smiled insincerely. "Let me know if you have any issues, won't you."

Meri chose today's expression. She arranged her features into almost catatonic idiocy, and gazed back, blank-eyed as a doll.

Yesterday, when the woman had berated her for her "poor attitude", Meri had selected "madwoman in the attic", all round-eyed and hollow-cheeked, showing her teeth, and had had the pleasure of watching the boss jerk and step away. Before the new appointment, Meri managed all regional political communications – with verve and panache and never missing a deadline. Now they expected her to still do all the work but put the new boss's name on it.

Meri blanked her mind and let the tirade wash over her. Pictured the beach – hmm, maybe she'd go for a visit this weekend. How she craved the ocean. How she *always* craved the ocean.

The manager bent further over the desk, assaulting Meri with a wave of synthetic rose parfum. "Are you listening to me?" she hissed, venomous as a death adder.

Meri flicked a nervous smile at her tormentor, picked up her sound-cancelling headphones and slowly put them on. She gazed at her computer screen, put out two fingers and began to type.

The woman yelled a little and stalked away.

Oh no! She'd latched onto a fresh victim: their new intern, an easy target. As the bully snarled, the grad's eyes grew shiny and his whole posture drooped. His voice wobbled as he muttered, "Yes Boss."

The manager flashed a smirk across the desks to her bully-apprentice, who snickered, relishing the signs of emotional pain in their victim.

Rage sparked through Meri's blood. She must do something.

Meri fixed her focus on that cup of coffee in the boss' manicured talons. She felt inside herself, connecting with the water in her blood, in her muscles, feeling it slip and slide inside her, outrage swelling her cells. The liquid began to slosh and swirl in the woman's coffee cup, to rock higher and higher, and then splaaaaaash! A torrent of dark fluid, at least three whole mugs, sloshed down her skirt and all over her fancy shoes.

Meri blinked, shock zapping through her body. *Did that actually work, Hamish?*

The manager screamed, waved her arms to ineffectively wipe coffee from her skirts, and knocked over the grad's water bottle, which somehow shot in the air to the bully-buddy's desk, immediately soaking all the papers, notebook, keyboard and computer screen, which fizzed and blanked to black.

He leaped up, lost his composure and swore at his mentor, at the same time sending his office chair scooting across the room to smash into Cranky

Sally, who glared in fury, and immediately began typing up a discrimination complaint to HR.

The boss whipped around and glared at Meri as though the whole mess was her fault (well fair play, it actually was) and tottered off to the bathrooms. Left in blessed freedom from harassment for five minutes, and hopefully longer if the woman went home to change, Meri focussed back on her deadlines.

"You are *fine*," she whispered to herself, squashing post-confrontation nausea and jitters. "Dream about magic instead."

That morning on the trail, a symphony of frogs burbled and croaked in the wetlands, like an office alive with gossip. She felt if she listened hard enough, she'd understand them.

Mad. Mad-mad-mad.

She had a science degree, for glory's sake. She dealt in data and facts and then spun them into written words that waltzed and delighted, persuaded, obscured and reframed. She could never speak such lovely lines though. In conversation, she agreed and stuttered and said half-things rather than what she wished she could somehow express.

She totally failed at office politics. Reading people? Huh. So often it felt like a foreign language. Worse, she lacked the dehumanising capacity to fawn and laugh at the director's jokes and listen raptly to his rambling until her brain froze over and life stretched before her like a dull, murky haze.

Yet, from the age of about fifty-two, she'd gradually been getting more herself, growing a bit of attitude at last, shocking everyone by saying what she really thought in meetings, and wearing what made her feel good.

Today, for example, she wore a bright pink and orange knee-length floral dress, hair elegant in a high bun, gold and pearl earrings – and socks and wide-fit sneakers. That way, she could stride around, walk briskly up the stairs, enjoy a lunchtime stroll in the sunshine.

She'd ditched "age-appropriate" as yet another tool to keep women about to step into their most powerful age yet – the third age – repressed and compliant. Well, blah to that.

At the same she was getting more herself, bits seemed to be falling off and malfunctioning: knees, molars, brain, lower back, feet.

Meri didn't let that stop her. She went to Club-bercise at the gym and danced, until she tore something in her knee and had to change back to weight classes; she wore bright colours and began sticking up for herself – such fun! *Why didn't she ever do it before?*

Maybe the loss of her husband Hamish, the grief forever stinging like a thorn in her heart, had fired her up. And so many of her old friends were moved away or tragically deceased now, floating in the universe or particles in the earth; embodied in dragonflies and crab apple blossom and sun-dia-monds on water.

What will she do with her one miraculous life?

Trouble was, now she was shedding her fears and rising stronger and fiercer like a phoenix, she didn't know who Merilea MacRury really was. What did she even really want? What were her real talents? Did she have gifts that she'd never nurtured and maybe should explore? What kind of friends did she seek? Was it all too late?

"Morning everyone!" Oh no. The director. Unfortunately, he'd caught Meri standing up at her desk. One, two, three...

"How's the weather up there, Merilea?" He looked up at her, then around the office, expecting the laughs. Sycophantic titters rippled. Encouraged, the director said, "We've lost network. Have you got a signal up there? Ha ha."

A voice shouted, "Can you see Uranus from up there?"

Meri gasped out, "Is that a bald spot on your head, sir?" She'd been practising brave responses. She refused to be complicit with these trolls any longer.

At least that was the plan.

Her height-challenged director's face purpled. His eyes burned hot as hellfire. His nostrils flared. "Get on with your work," he snapped. "Can't take a joke, can you? This attitude is why we put a manager over you—"

Meri imagined herself swimming in the ocean, the cool salt water carrying her high, a splendid rush of exhilaration as a curling wave carried her onto the sand. She imagined the roar of the ocean drowning out the words. Finally, the man stalked off to smirk and flirt with his freshly dressed crony. She swallowed against a dry throat, struggling to calm the quiver in her hands.

Don't let them make you small.

Despite her battle to stay positive and sane, a surge of hot, stinging tears leaked from her eyes and tracked down her cheeks. Face down, she scrubbed at her cheeks before anyone saw.

She would fly to wild Tasmania this weekend. How she yearned for rich rainforest and pristine beaches, how she longed for the sea, her cure-all.

Sooty Shearwater migration song

The long migration with my bird-kin is calling, calling, tugging in my muscles, singing within our shimmer of shearwaters. We rest in Uist, and Tree murmurs, tell this tale to Seal and Whale, and so I swoop out of the flight formation and ride the shapeshift whale's back and chirp the Plant Fae's message: please find her, blood of my blood, bone of my bone, and send her to me. The time is now.

Then with gladness pulsing in every wingbeat, I rejoin our shearwater shimmer, where the chill winds cannot reach us, protected by kin feathers, kin warmth. And on we fly.

Merilea inhaled chill, pristine air, her brain spinning headlines: "Visit the wild west coast of Tasmania, next stop Antarctica!" Freezing winds, cold seas, snow and sleet on the mountaintops in winter.

"Experience old-growth southern rainforests scented with four-thousand-year-old Huon Pines, the oldest trees on earth; see colossal pale-trunked Mountain Ash, the tallest flowering tree in the world." Lush green ferns of all sizes, dripping moisture. Deep, dark soils. True wilderness – some species in the south west wilderness had still not been named. She'd been bushwalking all yesterday, imbibing the luscious green healing and peace.

This morning, she awoke with the rose and gold dawn, sprang from bed, donned her cut-off wetsuit, sprinted down to the beach and dived into the surf. Oh, the shock of the cold! *Hello, I'm alive!*

She always stayed well within her depth. Australian oceans were full of terrors, varying with latitude: sharks, toxic jellyfish, stingrays, stone fish that could paralyse you, riptides that dragged you far out to nowhere, huge breakers that slammed you face first into the sand.

She swam and bodysurfed, joy soaring like a symphony as the waves held her high then rushed her to shore.

A strange song hummed in the air, a haunting, discordant music that brought Meri to a full stop. She stood in the shallows, ears straining to hear. Her heartbeat banged in her ribs.

Meri waded to shore and peered around the curve of the bay. Without conscious volition, she began to run, hobbling, slipping on the sand. The eerie music called and called. Urgency possessed her and drove her faster, despite needles of pain twanging in her hips and knees.

When she rounded the coastal dunes into the next bay, the most incredible sight met her dazed eyes.

A massive, unfathomable grey shape rolled in from the sea, landing high on the sand. More of them followed. Sounds of distress seared her, becoming higher pitched, pinging in her mind and chest. Her brain rang with emotion: confusion, fear, panic.

A whale stranding.

The animals were marvellous, majestic – and distressed.

Think, Meri! What did one do? Keep them wet with seawater. Call for help. Fook it, she never took her phone swimming, in case someone stole it.

Tears of despair pricked her eyes. She must run all the way back to her car, drive to her forest cabin and collect her phone, drive to where there was phone reception and call for help...meanwhile these wonderful beasts were suffering. Even as she stood there, awed at their majesty, never seen so close before, and panicking, wanting to assist, more whales stranded themselves, like a hideous, deadly orca game of sardines.

She turned to implement the only plan she had – it would take far too long – then suddenly, she spied a graceful silhouette out on the horizon. A surfer. Worried she'd further alarm the helpless whales, she ran back along the beach, then screamed and shouted and waved at the figure, until – she sobbed with relief – the person waved at her, and made its way towards her, the roar of the sea thundering in the salty air.

The surfer elegantly rode a wave all the way to the sand, flipped his board and tucked it under his arm. For a moment, Meri forgot everything in admiration at the grace of movement. Was she too old to learn how to surf? She'd always wanted to – why on earth hadn't she?

Another whale song of distress pinged in her mind. She ran to the surfer as he tugged off his hood, revealing long dark hair lit with silver above strong, craggy features.

She stared *up* at him. The man was *tall*. "Help! Look – stranded whales," she babbled, waving her arms. "Not for long, I just saw the first one, then

Hugo, the man as magnificent as the great whales, as wild and natural as the ocean. Imagine meeting him again. Maybe she could return to Tassie, to that beach...

But first, MacRury, you must discover – are you magic, or just deluded? Fairy blood! Cue laundry dance.

Was she one of those romantasy faes, with devastatingly handsome masked heroes and multiple lovers all adoring her? Or perhaps she'd be a cozy witch with a quirky coven of witchy friends who saved nature together.

What did you do, once you decided you had fae blood?

You took the advice of the mysterious surfer /ancient Norse warrior who appeared in time to the others followed, and oh no, look, the poor beasts are still coming, beaching themselves..."

The surfer pulled a phone from an invisible pocket, tapped at the screen, spoke urgently. He shoved his phone away and grabbed her shoulders. "Hey, whale maiden. I'm Hugo, a marine biologist, a professor with the uni." His deep, calm rumble slowed her panic. "Now don't worry, help is on the way. Bob Brown Foundation, marine rescue, volunteers, enviro groups. We've had too many whale strandings in recent times, but at least we all know what to do now."

The next few hours passed in a blur as Meri worked with groups of people to fill buckets with seawater and keep the mammals' skin wet, carefully avoiding their blowholes. Thankfully high tide began to roll in within the first hour. Organised teams of volunteers and emergency crews lined up along the whales and heaved and rolled them onto heavy canvas sheets and then hauled them back into the water. People wore a motley collection of clothing: pyjamas with raincoats; shorts and hoodies; wetsuits. They'd grabbed whatever was to hand and rushed to the beach to assist the whales.

Many, like Meri, cried often. People hugged and cheered every time one of the magnificent animals made it back into the sea.

New people appeared with coats, coffee, food, big towels, which Meri gratefully accepted. Her exposed arms and legs had purpled with cold.

Meri sought for her inner water magic. She struggled hard to call the waves higher and faster, frustration and urgency squeezing in her belly. Now would be a good time! But she couldn't find the spell. Her anxiety was too prickly, the ocean too limitless.

Suddenly, a rogue wave gushed into shore and carried a young whale calf safely back to the deeps. Had she magicked that super-wave? Or was she delusional?

Finding herself next to Hugo in one of the lines, feeling closer to these strangers than to most people, she suddenly confided, "I think I'm fae. I think I might have magic powers."

Argh. Did she really say that out loud to the athletic professor?

She shut her eyes. When she dared to open them again, trepidation burned in her throat. And realisation smote her in that moment – an expectation of ridicule and bullying had somehow become her norm.

Hamish, how did I let myself get to this? Level up, MacRury.

But Hugo didn't mock. He paused, bucket sloshing, regarding her gravely with his clear grey gaze. A wry smile danced on his mouth. "Surfing out there beyond the breakers, beyond the sunrise, I see, hear and feel things that have no explanation in heaven nor earth." He raised strong dark brows. "You came from nowhere and found the whales in the nick of time. What are your other fae symptoms?"

Warmth suffused Meri. She emitted a nervous laugh and huffed a breath. It felt so *liberating* to speak her crazy truth. "I...I'm amazing at navigation. Outdoors, I always know where I am, even in dense rainforest." She inhaled, held the breath, exhaled in a rush. "I hate perfume, can rarely take medicines, detest chemical smells, and weird things happen all the time. I *crave* nature, always. I must exercise or go mad."

Hugo threw another water bucket and stroked the whale's barnacled skin. "You might be autistic? On the spectrum? With all the sensitivities and compulsions, I mean."

"Um. Yep. That too probably." She blinked. He could be right. Autistic, not fae?

Her new friend grinned, white teeth gleaming in the soft Tasmanian light. He gently scratched off a whale barnacle. "So, congratulations on saying the fae thing out loud. And secondly, what are you going to do about it?"

"Do?" Meri laughed, then slowly sobered. "You mean, not just play silly tricks on office bullies? Actually...find out...more?" She frowned. "How would I do that?"

Hugo turned and cast a bucket of water over her legs, chuckling as she shrieked and leaped backwards. He leaned in. "Awake! Get a DNA test. Find your long-lost fae relatives and *learn*."

Meri aimed a full bucket at him, the water missing as he sprang away, his muscular surfer thighs giving him agility and power. They both laughed.

He stepped in close again and said, voice soft, "Trade for trade. I'm an ancient warrior, some kind of old Norse sea-aligned race." He thumped his chest. "I know it here—" He pointed between his dark brows, "—and here. So, I get it."

They locked gazes for a beat, in perfect accord, then silently went back to saving the whales. Shortly after, Meri lost Hugo in the crowd. He seemed to have vanished.

"That would be right," she mused. "A magic Norse warrior-surfer appears to guide me and then disappears." She knew the tales. Sometimes the magical guides were the helpers on your hero's journey, an Obi Wan for Luke; other times they were antagonists, sent to block or confuse your path.

She frowned. Maybe he'd invented the warrior story to make her feel safe?

Am I over-thinking it, Hamish?

Some of the whales they couldn't save. "Why do the whales strand themselves like this?" Meri asked, everyone asked each other.

Biologists from the University of Tasmania said, "Nobody knows. Changes in the ocean ecology, wrought by climate change and filthy, greedy fish farming practices. Whale harvesting conducted by foreign entities. Nuclear testing in the Pacific."

That Sunday night, Meri flew home to her regional city and her nasty job, hugging her Tasmanian adventure close in her heart. Something inside her had changed forever.

As she unpacked and washed her stuff, thoughts flew around in her brain like rainbow lorikeets squawking and squeaking. She'd heard the whale song as they inexplicitly and tragically stranded themselves. And yet the researcher told her that humans could not hear whale song from land.

And she'd worked with strangers to save many of the hunchback whale pod. People of a kind she never knew existed. Warm-hearted folk who cared about nature and wild things. People with whom – imagine – she might be friends.

What on earth had been doing with her life all these years? Why had she believed – for decades – that she just had to *endure*? Why had she not acted to *choose* the life she wanted?

What do you reckon, Hamish?

A thought slithered: had her beloved husband been part of the problem? She shook her head, briskly shaking out that unwelcome idea.

Now. Decision time.

Should she keep going in her current groove, too old, too safe, to change? Every year for decades – at forty two, fifty two – she'd believed she was too old, too late, couldn't afford it, yada-yada; yet here she was at sixty two, fully fit and functioning (excepting a few twinges here and there), brain still firing.

Or – she could grab a new trajectory, embrace her remaining years and create a life full of vividness and pleasure. Forget she was sixty two! Take action. Make choices. The idea sent warmth flowing through her like buzzy nectar, her brain glowing, a happy smile dancing on her face.

She plunged her beloved wetsuit in cold water to rinse it, wafts of sea and whale smell teasing her nose, bringing back the ocean, and the surfer...

guide you, for good or bad, and get DNA tested and then seek out your Scots fae ancestors and relatives.

Because, in her bones and blood, *she knew.*

The DNA test confirmed it. She was a proper, Scottish fairy. A *sidhe / sìthiche*. Her genetic code aligned. She belonged in the Outer Hebrides.

So what did you do? You jumped on a plane and ventured to those misty, lost islands and found your kinfolk, huddled on their windswept western islands, buffeted by vast oceans.

That's what you do.

You seek your truth.

CHAPTER TWO
Loch visions and a sinister shove

The flight from Melbourne to Edinburgh took twenty-four hours, squashed in economy, then Meri unravelled her cramped muscles with a lovely train journey to Inverness through the glorious Scottish countryside. In Inverness, she hired a car and drove to Ullapool in Wester Ross. She ate langoustines and drank a floral whisky chosen from the blackboard whisky menu, and next day took the first car ferry across the Minch to the Outer Hebrides.

Meri stood on the highest open platform, clutching the railing, revelling in the sea breeze on her face and the views changing to misty, melting

seascapes of blues, purple, mauve, pink, blending with sky and horizon. A pod of dolphins
leapt close to the vessel, and seals rolled and
dived in the breakers. Sea eagles, cormorants,
gulls swooped and called in the cerulean sky.
A tight knot inside her began to unfurl. Some
ancestral, genetic memory woke up, wallowing
in a strong sensation of homecoming.

Land appeared like a smile on the edge of the
world. The ferry arrived in a bustle of cars and
people on the isle of Lewis, the largest and most
northerly of the string of remote islands off the
western coast of Scotland. She waited in her car
and joined the queue from the ferry, set her sat
nav to Callanish on the western side of the island.
As soon as she was alone on the narrow road, she

pulled into an overtaking bay and opened the car door.

And then, at last, she set foot, in her extra-wide sneakers (bunions), on the magical Outer Hebrides, the land of her ancestors.

Shrieking seabirds ringed tall sea cliffs. Yellow and pink wildflowers shone like colourful fallen stars from grassy fields – the *machair*. Ancient granite boulders poked through weather-bent shrubs like the bones of her beginnings. The edges of everything wavered in a faint mist, as though enchanted.

Tears sprang into her eyes as she raised her arms to the sky. "I greet you! Hello lovely Outer Hebrides. Hello my ancestors, my lost culture, my lost language, my lost kinfolk."

She inhaled deeply, savouring the rich, complex smell that emanated from the deep peat soils, brine, salt air, and low heathy vegetation. Throat tight with emotion, she flung herself to the ground amongst the heather, and lay flat, arms out on the soil of her ancient kinfolk. Her fingers tightened on a smooth, hard object.

A car horn startled her. Meri leaped to her feet, face flaming. Her right knee wobbled beneath her; struggling for balance, her extra-wide shoe caught on a tangled root and she pitched over, arms flailing wildly, and fell straight into a prickle-filled bush. A demented shriek tore from her throat as her body exploded away from the prickles, landing her face first in the only mud puddle, she was sure, for fifty miles.

"Are you OK? Can I assist ye?" The deep male voice, heavily Scots-accented, rippled with suppressed laughter. A strong hand hooked under her arm and hauled her to her stupid feet. She stared, mortified, into a man's chest sprouting wiry black and grey hairs at the neckline, then raised her gaze to vivid blue eyes set in a weather-beaten, grinning face. "Whit were ye about, lass, laying there with your arms out, smelling yon peat? Ye're lucky a viper didnae take a nibble of you."

Viper? Meri squeaked, pulling herself away and nimbly leaping to safety onto the ribbon of bitumen snaking through the landscape. Feet now planted on solid roadway, thank all the old goddesses, she absently shoved the curved object in her pocket and scrubbed at her mud-splatted face.

"Th-thank you," she managed. Her gaze took in a battered farm truck, squeezed in behind her rental car in the narrow bay. "Um, jetlag, sorry...I'm from Australia. I'm Merilea MacRury. A very long time ago, my ancestors came from the Outer Hebrides. From...Uist. Is that how you say it?"

Her rescuer gave a short laugh, followed by a guttural, impossible sound, which she took to be the correct way of pronouncing "Uist". Luckily, he didn't expect her to repeat the sound, merely adding, "Oh aye? Verra welcome you are, lassie." A devilish smile curled his lips. He waved towards her bottom. "Need some help removing those wee thorns?"

"No," Meri replied in strangled tones, a hot blush searing her skin. "I seem to have escaped that indignity. Thank you."

He grinned, saluted, and drove away.

"Oh you fool!" A mad laugh escaped her throat. "What must he have thought, the poor man?" Snorting with sudden and irrepressible giggles, rubbing her bruises, Meri got back into her car, wiped the last of the mud from her face, checked the sat nav, and headed towards Callanish.

Another ten miles along, on impulse, she pulled into a tiny cafe attached to a small farmhouse, yielding to the lure of a refreshing cup of tea. The cafe proprietor had the same sparkling blue eyes, the same musical Scots accent as the man on the road, and great vivacity. By the time that redoubtable Scotswoman had plied Meri with a reviving cup of tea, home-made fruit cake, and a tourist map; taught her how to say "hello" in island Gaelic, and extracted a stunning quantity of facts and personal information from Meri in return, she felt sufficiently revived from her travels and travails to not waste another instant in heading to her Bed and Breakfast at Crulivig, and thence out to admire the famous Callanish Standing Stones circle in the evening gloaming.

"Here. You'll be needing these." Dolina, the cafe owner, winked and proffered a wrapped pack of baked goods.

Meri shook her head. "I couldn't fit another thing! But thank you. You saved my life with your delicious tea and cakes."

"Go on, dear. Give it to himself there at yon bed and breakfast to keep him sweet. A gift. And don't be a stranger; I'll see you soon." Her suddenly intent blue gaze pinned Meri. "I'm here if you ever need someone..."

Warmed with hospitality and new friendship, Meri followed the texted directions from her host, as *sat nav is eccentric here*, across wild, barren landscapes, arriving at a super-cute, double storey, whitewashed cottage nestled by the edge of a loch embraced by blue and purple-lit hills.

The loch, round as a bubble, mirrored the sapphire skies, dancing clouds, and the misty blues and mauves of the hills. "How lovely!" Meri enthused as she unfolded her cramped body from the car and went to stand at the water's edge. The colours in the loch swirled; shapes merged, broke and reformed into strange scenes: a face, an eagle, a battle, people wearing skins, silver armour...Meri stared, entranced, leaning closer and closer...

"You!" A deep man's voice shattered the spell. She jerked and almost lost her balance, arms flailing. The world tipped; her wide-eyed reflection stared back at her; just before she hit the water, a firm— horribly familiar! —fist gripped her upper arm and hauled her to safety.

"I might have known," the voice rumbled satirically in Meri's ears. "Do ye wish to fall in my loch, now?" He shook his head in what she considered an unnecessarily theatrical manner. "Tourists!" he muttered in a disgusted tone, crossing his arms.

A terrible embarrassment arose in her breast, mingling with a powerful urge to deliver a snappy retort. "I was fine until you startled me!" She snuck a glance back at the story loch. How strange. The pictures had calmed into reflections of the sky and the hills, the surface gently undulating with an invisible breeze.

He laughed, and murmured something that could have been, "Whisht, wee witch." She really should have got her hearing aids tuned before she travelled. Except most of the time she didn't wear them, just for work, conferences, musicals and opera. She lip-read and did a lot of guessing.

Meri regarded the man standing before her. Shorter than her, like most men. Mature, muscular, with a stubborn chin and penetrating gaze.

She screwed up her nose at his twisted grin, and turned to survey the darling whitewashed cottage, its windows and doors flung open invitingly as though smiling at her. Mollified, she demanded, "I'm looking for Murdo MacIver, my bed and breakfast host?" She pulled a face of exaggerated horror. "Surely, it cannot be yourself?"

That azure gaze flashed with mirth. "I could deny all knowledge and send you five miles further along the road. But that would nae be neighbourly, would it, to inflict a deranged tourist on the village?"

She glared. "No more nonsense, please! I'm Meri MacRury, and I've booked and paid for the *Bansìthe Bothan* holiday stay, and I've just travelled for *three days* from Australia to get here, and I lack exercise or proper food or sleep, and I...and I..." To her absolute chagrin, her throat thickened, and tears pricked at the back of her eyes. No! *Don't cry, Meri...*

The grin disappeared. His frown became a dreadful midnight glower. "Not Ban *Sith*."

She swallowed. "Not the Bansìthe Bothan?" Exhausted tears threatened to spill. Her voice scraped in her throat. "Where am I then?

"You are at the reet place—" Relief filled her. Until his next words. "—But its pronounced *banshee.*"

"I've booked *Banshee Cottage* for a week?" As though to underline her words, the small breeze eddying across the loch suddenly picked up, whirling around and echoing with a faint eldritch screech. Her rising panic escaped in mad hiccupping giggles. "I s-suppose I can stand by the loch and scream too, then."

His lips twitched and the dark glower morphed back into his trademark satiric grin. "Oh aye. But be careful you don't summon the *Ban-sìthe* to ye with all yon shrieking. The fae might come to claim you. They are well mischievous."

She stared round-eyed, half-appalled and half-intrigued. Was he teasing?

Before he could make another mocking remark, she remembered Dolina's prescient gift. The memory of her new friend's warmth gave her strength. "I have baked goods to give my host," she announced tartly, "Whomever he may be." She raised her brows.

Hope flared in his eyes. "Dolina's, aye?" At her nod, he growled, "Well I'm your host. Welcome."

He held out his hand for her car keys. She shot him a snooty look and opened the car boot herself. She leaned in for her luggage, but his stalwart arm was there before her, hauling out the suitcase and carry-on without even a grunt.

He shouldered the front door further ajar, ducked under the lintel, and led her into a charming, clean front room, painted white and decorated in a Scottish country style. Tartan rugs adorned the floor and draped over the couches. Paintings of Scottish countryside and nature graced the tartan-papered walls: sweet-faced hares, speckled white owls and delicate native flowers. Apart from the rugs and pictures, the room was spartan and masculine, with no knickknacks, simply a single bowl of yellow daisies.

Feeling instantly reassured by the prospect of cleanliness and comfort, her spirits restored, Meri followed his sturdy back up a narrow, twisting staircase to a pretty loft room, with views over the loch and the hills.

She stood in the middle of the room, emitting a gasp of pleasure.

"Mayhap I should change your room, to one with nae view of yon loch?" He was quizzing her, the beast.

The room and the view is lovely, thank you," she replied, returning his humorous grimace. "The landscape is so very pretty. Everything drenched in soft pastel colours, all those blues and mauves and pinks, all kind of misty and washed with water. So different from the harsh, vivid colours of Australia."

She caught a strange intent expression flash across his face, before his customary sardonic expression returned. He grunted, then resumed showing her the cottage: two bathrooms, with various amenities, a well-set up country kitchen, a pleasant, tiny garden on the loch side of the cottage with outdoor table and chairs.

He took her back into the kitchen and gave her a welcome cup of tea, arranging Dolina's cakes on a floral china plate and placing them before her.

He promised her he would return next evening and cook her a seafood dinner with shellfish and lobster "just off the ferry." She enthusiastically agreed to this. He growled, "Rest yeself now. If ye need anything, you have my number. And stay away from the edge of my loch!"

"Why, is it indeed a magic loch?" She grinned at him.

His countenance darkened, heavy brows snapping together. "Don't mess with what ye dinna understand," he muttered.

Rebuked, she sat back in her chair. Searching for another topic, and giving way to her curiosity, she asked, "Is there a Mrs MacIver?" Wishing to show inclusiveness, she added, "A Mr MacIver, perhaps?"

His frown gathered like a storm. His face stiffened, akin to the granite hills outside. His lips pressed white. Oh oh. There must be a tale here.

An imp of mischief stirred within her. "Never mind. I'll ask Dolina at the cafe." She was right. His gaze flashed blue fire.

He glared for an uncomfortable length of time. His voice rasped. "I tell you to stay away from the loch, because many long years ago, young Mrs MacIver was taken by the *Ban-sìthe* who visit the loch. She fell – or willingly jumped – in. And now she has joined their ranks, to scream and rattle at my door on storm-dark nights."

Meri's face froze in utter horror. She stuttered a few meaningless monosyllables. "Your wife?" she at last whispered. His chin jerked, possibly signalling agreement.

"I'm sorry."

Her host's glower intensified. His nostrils flared. He rose abruptly, gritting out the sounds as though forcing every word, "I'll be back to-morra night to cook seafood. Wee pie for ye for the night." He waved at the fridge. The door banged behind him.

Meri immediately became possessed by a strong urge to return to Callanish Cafe and discuss her mysterious, gothically tortured host with her new friend Dolina. She instantly wanted to know the whole tale: an accident? Or something more sinister. Did his lovely young wife suffer from a mental health disorder, schizophrenia, undiagnosed PTSD? She gripped the table.

Yet at the same time, a heavy lassitude filled her limbs and fogged her brain. She gave an enormous yawn. Jetlag had arrived, as undeniable as winter. Too dangerous to drive.

She dragged herself up the stairs, showered quickly, and fell insensible into a bed as high and soft as a cloud.

And if faint screaming whickered at the borders of her sleeping brain, she barely heard it.

She awoke blearily with golden light shining around the edges of her curtains. She rose and peered out. The loch glimmered in the ghostly half-light, reflecting golds and pinks swimming in the sky. Distant gold-lit hilltops transformed into magic beacons. Mauve and purple shadows lurked in hollows and smudged every form in the landscape, changing the terrain. She touched her phone screen: good grief, ten pm!

She splashed water on her face, dressed, and headed downstairs, the gloaming calling to her like a song from long ago, plucking at deep chords in her mind.

Oh, how magical! She stepped towards the loch, watching the vivid reflections ripple in its strangely shifting surface. That had been so weird earlier, those odd visions; no doubt a figment induced by jetlag.

Now, she raised her arms high and stretched her body, embracing the whole experience: the gloaming, the harshly beautiful landscape, the hills, the loch, the scents of heather and peat. She sighed a huge, happy sigh and spun in a circle, stopping when dizziness threatened to tip her to the ground.

She took a step closer to the loch, and closer, until she stood at its stony edge, little rills of water almost lapping at her sneakers. She leaned over, her hands on her knees, peering into the blue and purple depths.

She gave a small shriek: was that a pale face? A white hand, *beckoning to her*? In her mind, Hamish said sternly, *Don't be silly. You know you are imaginative and suggestible.* And yet...could that be a sword, embellished with coloured jewels, its haft ornate, like a medieval treasure? And a...

A hard shove landed between her shoulder blades. She cried out in shock; her arms windmilled, seeking balance, and then with a great splash, she landed in the loch. Blue and gold speckles exploded around her like fireworks in the water, distorting her vision; then the water settled.

Cold. Wet. Her cotton tracksuit quickly became sodden and weighty. She tumbled around, disoriented, panic fighting with her urgent need to breathe.

Her hand slipped into her pocket. Her fingers touched the smooth object; a weird certainty filled her. *Water was her element. She adored swimming.* She moved her arms until she saw light bouncing on the surface, then kicked her legs hard to send her upward, inhaling a great, grateful breath when her face met sweet air.

She glanced at the object still clutched hard in her frozen left hand. A curved tooth, maybe some kind of water mammal: how strange – and how lucky. She slid her talisman back into her wet pocket.

Prickling with alertness, she tread water and peered back to shore, seeking her assailant, her heart thudding. Nobody. Had she imagined that heave?

There! A figure striding fast along the loch path towards the village. The dark silhouette was broad and masculine, horribly similar to her host's. Fear screamed in her brain like the music from *Psycho*. Had she chosen the holiday stay managed by *a serial murderer*? Her mind clanged like a bell of doom, repeating, *like his wife, his wife, her life.*

Terror grabbed her brain. More fears rushed in: what creatures swam in this loch? She peered anxiously into the translucent depths. No doubt crystal clear in the sunlit day, now the water shimmered pink and gold and mauve in the gloaming, sleek shadows swimming in the depths. For a split second her mind showed her toothed prehistoric fish, predatory beasties, drowned faces...*Stop that!*

For a moment torn between the imaginary horrors lurking in the loch and an unknown, yet corporeal assailant possibly waiting on the narrow path, her brain cowering and her muscles quivering, her rational self at last galloped to the rescue.

Get out before you freeze or drown!

She should rush back to the cottage, pack up and leave. Sleep in the car, catch the morning ferry back to the Scottish Highlands mainland.

She swam and waded to shore, with no ancient water beasties biting her, and only two or three possible strokes from ghostly fingers – hopefully just waterweeds. She forced herself not to look down.

But when she at last stood on solid ground, shaking with cold and shock, fury ignited in her belly and burned along her veins. That fiend! These fat-feet, support sneakers were expensive! She began walking back to the cottage. Stopped.

How dare he give her such a fright! She pivoted. Stared into the direction her attacker had gone. Now waves of heat sizzled in her brain, her face burned hot and flushed, anger simmered like a cauldron in her belly. She could pursue the culprit and demand he pay for new ones.

She took off at a run, squelching along in her sodden sneakers, wet cotton slapping her body, to give her unknown assailant a piece of her mind. There! A glimpse of a gnarly male form.

Mad thoughts circled: why would MacIver push her in the loch? Was he re-enacting his wife's death with select summer visitors? Just how many bodies lay rotting in that loch—

No! *Don't think about that.* Given her clothes were drenched in loch water.

She quite enjoyed the run, the water in her shoes actually providing more support. Yet after half a kilometre, her pinging knees reminded her that she was sixty two; her limbs thought it was likely past her bedtime; and her brain, finally getting a word in, suggested chasing a serial killer on a distant island far from police and any person she knew, might not be the best idea for her continued survival.

She stopped, chest heaving, peering into the darkness.

Her fury had dissolved with the vigorous exercise. Fear tickled in her nerve endings. What on earth was she doing? And then terror grew wings and she found herself sprinting, gasping aloud, desperate to reach the relative safety of the cottage—

Slam!

She'd collided with something hard, warm, muscular—

"Oh my!" she screeched. Her hands groped wiry upper arms. "You feel human, at least."

A laugh curled around her ears. Firm steady hands settled on her shoulders. The familiar gravel tones of her host said, "Merilea MacRury? Its myself. Murdo MacIver."

Oh no. Horror battled with embarrassment and relief. She was torn between falling sobbing on his chest or snapping his head off with a few fear-spiked pithy phrases.

Before she could do either, he gave her arms and shoulders a rub with those capable hands, which was frankly quite enjoyable. He rumbled, "But why are ye soaking wet? It's not for me to criticise my tenant's actions, but yon loch is terrible cold and if you must swim, the daytime is preferred."

Meri wrenched herself from his grip and glared up at him. "Why am I drenched in potentially toxic loch water?" Fury erupted. "I know it was you. Pushing me in the loch! Fine way to welcome visitors, *not*! Are you entirely mad?"

She inhaled a few angry breaths. "You pushed me into that freezing pond, and then you waited, and leaped out at me like a...like a...sinister Hebridean serial killer."

He laughed, but his puzzled, wounded tone was plain. "Why would you think such a thing of me?"

She paused. *Don't say it. Don't say it.*

She said it. "Your...your w-wife. I thought you were...reenacting..."

"Are you making a mockery of my wife's death? My tragic lost bride?"

"No! Nononono...no," she squeaked, appalled.

"Well now." He smiled at her – thank goodness – in the gold-mauve half-light. "How about I take you back and give you a wee medicinal whisky. Good to keep out the chill – and any mad gremlins bouncing around in that charming head."

Charming head, charming head, echoed a feminine part of her. Her skin woke up.

As they walked back along the loch, she said, accusation sharp in her voice, "If you didn't push me, who did? For someone did."

"Forgive me, but ye mun be mistaken, lass. Did you lose your balance? The gloaming changes perspective, distorting distances and coating objects in shadows."

Ha! Not a chance. "Highly unlikely. I am very sporty and active. I do yoga. I know where my body is in space."

They strolled in silence for a beat, then he said, "The neighbours may be eccentric, aye, but they're not murderous. I suggest you show caution around foreigners."

Foreigners! Huh. They walked back in silence to the cottage, Meri half-glad of his protection, and half-terrified he would throw her back in the loch and finish the job.

In the event he did neither. Instead, he helped her check the entire cottage for imaginary intruders and weak security points, waited while she showered away the loch, then when she came downstairs, bestowed a lovely heathery medicinal whisky on her.

He smiled at her. "While you are here, you must see our famous Callanish Stone Circles. The large central circle, and the other three stone circles dotted through our landscape.

"Tomorrow! I can't wait. They look incredible online. So infused with power and crackling with magic."

In reply, Murdo shot her a gimlet gaze, then smoothed his features into blankness.

He stood, gave her shoulder a gentle squeeze, took both their glasses and put them on the sink. "Lock the door if ye wish – there is nae need, not in these Islands – and sleep tight."

After Murdo MacIver departed, Meri went around and double checked that everything was actually secured, her knees complaining and jabbing with every step.

She repeated like a mantra, that malicious push was nothing, nothing. Just a prank played on a summer tourist. Nothing to worry about. You probably imagined it.

She pushed a large piece of furniture across the front door and poured herself another small glass of the local whisky thoughtfully left by her host.

She held the crystal decanter up to her lips...and hesitated. Poisoned whisky?

Don't be mad! Everything is fine. She took a big swallow and waited for the death throes. Instead of toxic twitches, a very pleasant mellow sensation stole through her limbs.

So she took another sip.

She had choices, she mused. She could set her mind to pragmatic and firmly ignore everything odd and weird, just as she'd done *her whole life* – or she could open her mind, welcome in every mad idea, revel in each bizarre experience, celebrate every dreamlike vision, and generally enjoy herself.

She didn't even need that second glass of whisky.

She chose magic.

Because that's why she'd come all this way.

Filled with liquid courage, she went upstairs and fell into bed, to sleep deeply in a dream-state brimful of visions and marvels.

CHAPTER THREE
Isobel - A Fae from Uist and the Western Isles

"Bone of my bone, kin of my kin, I summon you." Isobel raised her arms, fingers spread wide in the gilded dawn.

Mist, thick and white, threaded with faint colours and ghostly shapes, hovered over the water-soaked landscape. Shining lakes stretched out before her, far as the eye could see, many lakes, all joining up and part of the watery scene. Pastel streaks rippled through the daybreak sky: peach, pink, yellow, green, purple blue, reflected like a second sky in a magical otherland in the lakes.

Water birds – herons, gulls, oystercatchers – stalked and flew over the water, huddling in groups or posing in proud solitary vigilance. A rare corncrake rasped invisibly from a clump of reeds.

The fairy ring Pobull Fhinn perched high on the side of the hill, facing west. Its stones were worn now, some tumbled and half-hidden in the heather; yet power still vibrated and resonated, magnified by the gleaming lakes and pink-streaked skies. Power which could still be summoned, by those of the ancient blood.

Isobel stood in the centre of the ancient fairy ring Pobull Fhinn and held her arms to the sky. She filled her lungs with the exquisite fresh, chill air of the fairy hills, and her mind with the scents and sights of the landscape around her. She was the landscape. It filled her, possessed her, ran rich in her veins.

Then she called to her kin: blood and bone, muscle and cells. Blood of her family, her ancestors, her nieces, all the daughters of her line. She called to the one: she had the pattern of that one's blood now, she could *feel* her here in the islands, call to her, make her blood prick and itch and want to move, drive, walk to Uist, the heartland of her origins.

It was time.

Everything depended on it.

"Merilea MacRury, of clan MacLeod, I call you, my daughter. I call blood of my blood, bone of bone, heart and mind, muscle and sinew. Come now, come home, at last. Come to your heritage and power. Come to the Way of the Sidhe." Isobel held her arms wide, let her heart and mind soar, let the power lift her.

She moved her hands, and the mist swirled, knotting itself into ghostly shapes. Far below, in the lakes, the images gained strength and colour.

Carefully, Isobel built the vision in the lake from reflections, sunlight and sparkles.

Far below, shimmering in the lake, the image of another fairy ring wavered and took shape. A grand ring, its huge stones taller than a man, with a central crossed aisle added later by the meddling Christians. Within the central avenue, a tall woman walked, her face alive with astonishment and wonder, a tentative finger stroking the stones.

Her cloud of dark red hair, heavily streaked with silver, glinted in the early sun.

With a snap of her wrist, Isobel flicked the summoning to Leòdhas, to her inheritor walking within the Callanish ring.

She waited.

In the rippling lake vision, the woman stopped, jerking her chin around as though sensing a presence. Instead of welcoming the sending, of embracing the magic, she jerked back, eyes wide, body crouched in a hunted, defensive posture.

Isobel sighed. Well. At least the *sìthiche* could feel her.

She was about to smooth away the vision, turn away, when a male figure strode within the Leòdhas fairy ring. Him! And worse! The woman she had gone to all this trouble of calling, summoning, and sending the vision to, turned, smiled at their enemy and walked to join him in the entrance to the central avenue.

Entrance, Isobel thought. Also functioning to en-*trance*, as her relative walked the fairy ring portal. But now, all Isobel's magical effort was blown to dust.

Just before the vision dissipated, the man stiffened. For one tense moment, his face looked directly at her from the lake vision, his Viking blue eyes lit with mockery; then he flicked his hand, ripples coursed over the lake surface and the sending vanished.

Murdo MacIver of Leòdhas, the most powerful warlock of the Western Isles.

Of course, he'd feel Merilea's magic. *Of course* he'd want it for himself, for whatever fell purpose the man had cooked up now. No doubt he'd already pushed her into his enchanted loch, to see the strength of her magic in gold and blue sparkle-dust.

Dam, blam, flam.

She *needed* an inheritor. She needed kin, so she could pass on the sacred duty of keeping the old ways, of caring for their island nature magic.

Because she could feel her *sìthiche* magic waning, wearying with age, dying now; and herself with it.

Meri stood in the most water-soaked landscape she had ever beheld, even for an Aussie, accustomed to long, wild coastlines and reed- and bird-filled wetlands. The fields floated in blues and greens, mists and clouds, dotted with pink, yellow and mauve wildflowers like fairy gifts. Black and white gannets and gulls screeched overhead.

The urge that had tugged her all the way from western Victoria to the bleak, remote, enchanting Outer Hebrides vibrated strongly here.

The Call. If she was magic, this is where she belonged, right here. Meri scrunched up her nose. She also belonged, heart and mind, to the wild rugged landscapes of glorious Australia and to its proud, reckless, kind-hearted people: that was her too.

So long ago, her ancestors adventured from these rugged Hebridean islands, risking all to travel to an unknown continent on the southern rim of the world, to make new lives. And they'd thrived. How proud she felt of her kin in that moment.

Here in this stone circle, one of the smaller Callanish Rings, the old magic was strong. She felt awed, and wonderstruck, and like she could breathe at last; quite desperate to know the names of all the birds skidding and floating and diving on the lakes; to learn the botanical names of plants and their uses, their magical properties; to acquire that language of magic, of alchemy, of ancient knowledge carried in the coding of her cells.

She sensed a presence. Intruding here, on her meditation.

She whipped around. Nothing. Uneasiness crawled on her skin. She jerked her head from side to side. Nothing.

Then she felt...someone...coming. She imagined a force field, a hard bubble all around her. "Begone!" she muttered. "begone!" She curved her arms in huge outwards shooing motions. "Go!"

The step came closer, a pebble skittering, but no person could be seen. Should she escape this stone circle? Run back to her car?

No. She was staying here in the fairy ring. *Be brave, remember?*

With all her focus, she imagined a spongy bubble encasing her, that took missiles and bounced them back out again like a giant fitball. The steps came nearer; she imagined spines on that side, nasty long spikes to shred any evil intent coming her way.

"I see what you are doing!" The words were followed by a cackle. Meri whipped around again.

A very tiny, silver-haired, bright-eyed woman stepped into the Fairy Ring. Her wide grin could only be described as mischievous. Her edges flickered and wobbled. A faint swirly mist curled in ribbons around her.

Meri's eyes practically burst from her skull. Her throat was so tight only a stuttery croak squeezed out. Half of her brain screamed, *run!*, But the other, braver, curious part, thought, *Am I speaking with a Scottish sìthiche?*

"You think that paltry bubble-shield will deter me? That it will hide you?" The tiny woman stepped closer. Power emanated from her in waves, almost visible in oranges and yellows. "At least you can make one even in the fairy ring. But ooh ye have a long way to go, lass."

Meri swallowed. Could this be Isobel...? Or indeed a *sìthiche*. The place could be riddled with them, for all she knew.

What the hell! She was here to learn, to take risks, to stick her neck out of its soft, comfortable collar. "Are you..." She screwed up her lips, moving the tight bud from side to side. "Are you Isobel MacLeod, *sìthiche*, and my relative?" she said in a rush.

The mischievous grin transformed into a gentle, warm smile which melted all Meri's fears. "That I am, wee lass. And a feisty one ye are! Look at ye! So tall and slender and strong." And the woman held out her stick-thin arms, and when Meri walked straight into the embrace, hugged her tightly. It was like embracing mist.

"There's only you, now," Isobel said. "Ye are the last, mebbe. We haven't much time." She stroked Meri's arm. "Unless the Others decide to stop their playing and come to join us."

"Others?" Chills slid up and down her spine.

"Aye, wee lass. Others. Mebbe there's some left." She squinted up at Meri, mischief dancing in the same cerulean blue eyes of most of the islanders. "Ye like to swim, aye? Then mayhap ye'll get to say hello."

Meri frowned, but Isobel refused to elaborate further.

The image wavered. "Come to Uist, my sweet. Come tomorrow." The spectre or sending or whatever she was began wavering in and out.

"But where...how shall I find you?" Meri asked desperately.

"Ye'll know," the wizened fairy said, before completely fading into the fairy-wrought mist.

That mist alone was a handy trick. Imagine pulling that back in the office.

So tomorrow, she'd drive to Uist. Urgency and fascination fought in her chest. A kind of high singing soared in her mind.

As she strode to her car, body light and fluid, her mind filled with music, she suddenly identified the emotion causing such sensations in her body and mind. Happy! She was *happy*! How long since she'd felt truly, wonderfully, magically happy?

Murdo MacIver dropped his half-finished cake on Dolina's outside table and strode to his car. By the time he reached the small Callanish Ring, whatever magic had pulsed in his cells like an alarm was long gone. He sniffed. Yes, a great magic had been worked here. His nostrils flared.

The trace of enchantment dissipated into sunlit speckles as a throng of mundane tourists milled into the main Callanish Ring across the field, oohing and aahing as they stared at the stones. Some of them even emitted tiny sparks of ancestral Scots magic, like fireflies. Not really enough to harvest. He'd bet they had no idea; they probably just thought they'd had a lucky streak or were *manifesting* or something.

His lip curled. No, there was only one good source currently on these islands.

He was giving her dinner tonight.

CHAPTER FOUR
New Friends

Meri anticipated with delight her seafood dinner planned for that evening, and more talk with the handsome, enigmatic Murdo MacIver. But as she stood in the tiny bathroom washing her face, an image wavered and formed in the mirror. Isobel! The elderly woman looked pale, as though the effort was sapping her strength.

Meri reached out a hand to the vision. "Isobel!"

The fairy's moved but no sound came. Meri put her hands either side of the mirror, held her face close. Hard to lipread when the other person had an accent.

"Stay away – from *himself*!" Isobel might have mouthed. "Come here to Uist *now*. Don't delay." Her gnarled hands made urgent beckoning gestures towards her own chest. No mistaking her message there!

When the vision faded, Meri stood, somewhat at a loss. Surely she was imagining all this? The Isobel visions? Besides, how she adored seafood! Tempting visions of succulent prawns and glossy lobster arose in her mind.

She paced around the bathroom. It was only a wait of another hour, she could go tomorrow, as planned, when she was fresh to drive. And surely Isobel could have used the *phone*?

She took three steps downstairs to await Murdo. An image swam in her mind: panic flashing in her elderly relative's pale face. She paused. She'd never met Isobel, except in visions. How did she know it was even her?

But she had to believe, or what was she even doing here?

Meri ran back upstairs, packed her bags in a rush, and guilt pinching like a lobster claw, left a rueful note on the table for Murdo. She consoled herself with the knowledge that he thought all tourists were mad anyway.

She tugged her luggage outside and piled it into the car. The sky and air hinted at the purple-golden gloaming to come. Meri stared around. Surely she'd imagine pixies and sprites in the eerie light?

She hesitated. It was a four-hour drive to her destination. With breaks, she might make it by nine pm.

Her glance caught the loch, glowing weirdly in the gloaming. Hmm, yep, OK. Time to head to Uist and hope that Isobel was, in fact, expecting her.

The drive was utterly glorious. Tall cliffs glistening with sea spray yielded to vistas of rolling green hills dotted with sweet white-washed cottages unfolding with every curve of the road. The evening progressed and the violet-gold gloaming lay over the landscape like a spell.

Weirdly, aged, mossy signposts seemed to spring up at intervals along the roadside, declaring *Iso-*

bel MacLeod's cottage this way! And *Not far now.* And even, *Not that way, fool!*

The amount of water in the landscape increased, large reed-edged lochs weaving in and out of each other, birds of every variety screaming and circling in the orange sky.

A long, narrow bridge took her to Uist. Arms shaking with exhaustion, Meri at last found the little cottage perched on the edge of a ribbony loch, near a small woodland which edged a three-storey, white-painted old-fashioned hotel. She pulled onto the gravel strip by the flower garden at the front of the cottage, unfolded herself from the car, stretched all her kinked muscles, and knocked at the door.

Nerves tickled and thrilled. What if this whole thing was the product of a crazed mind? Why did she think Isobel even lived here?

No answer.

Merilea MacRury, what in blazing hells have you done now?

She waited, knocked, waited. Finally, she trudged around to the hotel, and with considerable knocking and hallooing, managed to rouse a manager, a cranky-looking chap apparently entirely clad in tartan and body hair.

"Oh thank you!" Meri enthused. "May I have a room for the night? I've just driven from Callanish—"

"Weel tha's a fool and no mistake."

"I beg your pardon?" Meri blinked. Could she have heard aright?

"Ye drive four hours during the fairy time, I mun ask mesel', are ye bewitched, lassie? I see no car, indeed. I'd be a fool to allow ye within my duir. And ye should be askin' yerself, is this hotel fella in fact a hobgoblin?" He frowned, his enormous grey brows bristling like an offended caterpillar.

A giggle burst from Meri. "I'm so tired, hobgoblin or not, I'd welcome a room for the night." An idea struck her. "My relative—" she waved in the direction of Isobel's cottage, "Isobel MacLeod is expecting me."

His face effected so many startling changes at this news that Meri was hard-pressed not to give a shout of rather hysterical laughter.

"Hersel'? Aye, then, come within, come in," he said in a grumbling manner.

"She expected me tonight," Meri confided as she followed her host's bent tartan-clad form into the hotel. "But she doesn't seem to be there."

The hobgoblin whirled with a suddenness that elicited a small, embarrassing scream from Meri. "The Lady does as she does," he answered sternly.

Meri nodded as though chastised but failed to entirely suppress a squeak, which melded mirth and nerves.

Her host made a scratchy sound in his throat that might have even been a laugh.

In the end, the Hobgoblin Hotel, as Meri mentally termed it, turned out to be both clean and comfortable and delightfully old world. Her host

Donald MacNeil plied her with whisky and Scottish smallgoods of smoked fish, sausages, bannocks and cold swedes, which he called neeps. It all tasted delicious, and she tumbled gratefully into her high, soft bed not long after.

Meri woke fully at first light, threw off her feather doona, donned PJs and bounced over to the window, to let in more delicious pearl-honey early light, and to inspect the landscape in which she had found herself.

The dark green woods, full of pines and evergreens, still held night cloaked within their branches. The huge sky was lit with bright gold and rose, drifting clouds streaked with violet, mint green, tangerine: a hallelujah sky. She opened the window; fresh, crisp air beguiled her nostrils. She heaved in several breaths, exulting in the leafy scents.

She checked her watch. Almost five am. She washed her face, put in her eye drops, dressed quickly and warmly, putting her curved tooth-talisman in her pocket, then cautiously crept down the stairs.

The heavy front door fought her for a while, but Meri wasn't gym-fit for nothing. With a muttered curse, she managed to heave the door open and squeeze through the gap before it shut firmly behind her. Whoops.

Hopefully the hobgoblin would be awake by the time she came back. He'd promised her "full Scottish breakfast". Her stomach gurgled in anticipation.

Meri walked briskly down the rough gravel drive and around the edge of the woods towards the lochs, hills and Isobel's cottage, her eyes blinking wide in wonder. Cold air seared her nostrils. Orchestral music trilled in her brain. The landscape was half water and hills, half sky ribboned with colour.

A weatherbeaten wooden signpost scratched with the words *Pobull Fhinn* pointed to a skinny track through the heather which meandered up the hill. Meri followed it, watching out for snakes, an unbreakable habit for every bush-loving Australian. She rounded a corner and there it was.

An ancient standing stone circle stood imbedded in the west face of the hill. Light danced on yellow and grey lichens. Several standing stones had fallen, but enough were standing to create the strong sense of a magic circle, a ring of power.

So that's what a *ring of power* was. A standing stone circle, not a piece of jewellery.

Filled with awe and trepidation, Meri stepped into the fairy circle. Sensation rushed through her: a golden pulsing like magic, energy, power, conviction – and welcome. Like it knew her, called to her, bathed her in homecoming energy.

Meri stayed in the circle for an inestimable length of time. She lost track of past and future, left her body, lost her identity. She became the circle, the landscape, the water, the sky...

When she regained herself, blinking, she followed the twisting track up the hill, and from the summit, surveyed water laying in great sheets across the island, alive with waterbirds. Way below, she spied the tiny cottage nestled in a curve, her own car parked in front.

She rushed down the hill, checked her car and belongings were safe, then taking a deep breath, knocked on the door.

No answer, she waited; knocked again, and it opened under her hand. She paused. Was this fairy magic, the door opening apparently aided? Or something more sinister? And was this even Isobel's cottage? Maybe she'd be arrested for breaking and entering.

Licking her suddenly dry lips, eyes alert, she pushed the door and stepped over the threshold, the old fairytales of magic beings needing an invitation to step over your threshold thrumming in her brain.

The cottage echoed with silence. A cute front room opened into a hall which ended in a kitchen. Meri stood and stared at the overturned chair, the half-eaten breakfast, eggs congealing on a floral plate, a half full cup of coffee. Well at least fairies drank coffee! She hoped. She had feared she'd need to undertake some extreme diet to cleanse her body and mind while fairy training...

Focus! Maybe if she returned to the hotel, ate breakfast, and came back again in a while. Meri walked outside, closing the door behind her, inhaling with joy the scents of woodland and loch, rich peaty soil and garden flowers.

In the distance, the curve of ocean glimmered. Nearby, a dirt track appeared to lead straight there. Meri never could resist the sea! She checked her watch: six am. Plenty of time. She power-walked along the track, and after about a kilometre, was rewarded with a tiny cove: the ocean swathed in vivid blues: cerulean, topaz, turquoise, sky blue; edged with creamy, lacy breakers.

A pod of grey spotted seals surfed the waves, rolling and tumbling apparently for sheer joy of the day and the ocean. "My sea-loving sisters!" Meri called aloud in a sudden fit of madness. "I greet you! I greet the lovely ocean! Once I've met Isobel, I'll be back to swim with you." Swim in her trusty cutoff wetsuit. The sea would be freezing around these islands.

She squinted as a seal lazily waved a flipper. Hmmm.

OK, coffee was urgently needed; she raced back. The Hobgoblin Hotel door was propped open, and enticing breakfast smells emanated from a front room. In short order, the hobgoblin presented her with toast, poached eggs, bacon, Lorne sausage, black pudding, tattie scones, a slice of haggis, and baked beans. She demolished the lot, along with orange juice and two cups of strong, freshly brewed coffee.

That burgeoning sense of something wrong – Isobel didn't seem the type to miss appointments, but maybe serious, urgent magic of some kind was keeping her away – unfurled and tickled and scratched inside her.

Washed and dressed, Meri returned to the loch edge below the Pobull Fhinn fairy circle, on the edge of woodland.

Maybe she'd try a bit of landscape magic, water magic. Staring out where loch met sky in blurred misty blues, she raised her arms high with each deep breath. "Isobel where are you? Has something happened?" As an offering, akin to the ancient Celtic practice of throwing a precious gift into water, she threw in the tooth.

Meri closed her eyes and *felt* all the water in the landscape. The loch, the ocean, the lakes, groundwater, the sap running in plants, in her own body...power surged, with joy and some-

thing strong and vivid like she had never felt before – akin to punching out the best cardio and
weights workout of her life. Or catching the perfect wave: that surge of power and exhilaration...

She fell out of it. Nothing. The feeling died.

As she walked back to the cottage, hoping Isobel had returned and then Meri would be embar-
rassed by her own apparent tardiness—

Her brain stopped in its whirl of excuses. There,
besides a slender, white-trunked birch tree, just
by the cottage, drooped a woman: almost a trick
of the light. She was transparent, shimmery, as
thin and beautiful and medieval as a Burne-Jones
Camelot figure in a tapestry, clad in draping, flowing, shimmering garments which shifted with the
light.

Meri stopped, transfixed, then hurried over, for who knew how long the vision would last? "Hello," she said softly, creeping close enough to marvel at the creature's ephemeral beauty. "Have you come to lead me to Isobel?"

"Taken," murmured the creature, her voice as bubbling and musical as a brook tinkling over stones. "Taken."

Meri's heart began to thud. "Where? Who?"

As though she'd asked too many questions, the creature began to fade.

"Please, stay!" Meri pleaded. Oh no, had her voice had sounded too harsh? The creature had semi-disappeared in a burst of sunshine. "Help me, sweet lady," she begged.

"Taken,   taken...magical work...house...drain...mag..."

And then there was nothing there but a lovely tree, a shaft of sunlight dancing on its alabaster bark.

Horror filled Meri. *Taken*. "Am I mad? Hallucinating? Or has something happened to Isobel?" She rushed to the cottage, knocked, entered, and looked around once more. The half-eaten breakfast still sat on the kitchen table. Should she clean it up? Or leave it for the police?

Meri knew now it was Isobel's cottage, for the hobgoblin confirmed it. He also bade her not to interfere in the Lady's business, his bushy brows clumping together like agitated hairy caterpillars.

To calm her anxiety and indecision, she made a bargain. She'd go for a swim in that cute cove, then return. If Isobel was still missing, she'd talk to her host again, consider ringing the authorities.

Clad in her springer wetsuit, Meri surveyed the wild ocean before her. Always a bit dangerous to swim alone in unknown seas – but she was accustomed to that; Hamish had never swum with her. Ocean swimming was her own cure and heal-all for everything.

She checked the surface for rips and currents. It looked heavenly, the salty, heaving call summoning her. She waded out, checking the pull of the current against her legs; all fine, just a moderate tug, nothing to pull her all the way to America or Greenland. The water was only gently chilly, about the same as her own Victorian beaches in spring. She peered underneath the sea: no obstacles, and above, no fins lurking with menace waiting to crunch on her bones; for that matter, no ancient battles full of swords and blood.

Waves crashed and foamed over her. She could wait no longer and dived headfirst into the next breaker, laughing aloud as she fully immersed herself in the enlivening sea. Rising from the wave, water streaming from her body, she waved at the pod of seals surfing nearby, surfing the waves, rolling and diving. Cautiously she swam nearer and nearer, attracted by their abundant joy of ocean swimming, so similar to her own.

She watched the next perfect curl of a wave coming, waited until just before the dip, and swam with all her strength towards the shore. The wave lifted her, carrying her face and torso high out of the wave as it sped as fast and wild as her maddest ideas towards the beach. The wave flung her along the sand, grazing her palms, thighs and knees, but she only laughed as she leaped to her feet and ran high-kneed back into the water to catch the next one.

As she caught the wave, a silky, muscular shape cannoned into her, lifting her higher into the wave; together, they barrelled towards the shore, half-airborne, squealing and laughing with joy.

Meri was flung on the sand in the shallows once more, but the seal executed a fluid manoeuvre and was already back in deeper water, leaping out of the sea and barking at her, patently bidding her "hurry up!"

Meri and her seal-sister rolled and tumbled in the waves, body-surfing the long breaks, revelling in the buoyancy and vigorous freshness of the sea.

At times, Meri forgot she was a human woman and dived under the waves with her soul-sister, biting at coloured fish then exploding back up into the air.

Finally, her limbs shaking with exhilaration and exhaustion, Meri waded back to shore. A wave smashed her down; when she rose, a woman waded next to her, laughing, wiping salt from her eyes.

"Where did you come from?" Meri scanned the landscape and the sea: no towel on the sand, no water craft...

The woman had large brown eyes, ringed with thick black lashes, broad shoulders and a muscular body. She beamed with happiness. She said something in a guttural yet musical language: Scots Gaelic?

Then her new friend laughed again and said, "That was fun, wasn't it?" Either in English, or Meri could suddenly understand Gaelic. Nothing would surprise her in this ancient, magical land.

Her companion's words suddenly penetrated. "What was fun?" Meri essayed.

The woman nudged her playfully. "You aren't a bad surfer at all, for a human." She strode athletically next to Meri to shore, and beaming with another huge, happy grin, said "What are we doing next?"

Meri blinked. Was this woman the seal she had played with? Old stories of selkies rushed through her mind. "S-selkie?" It was like Meri's brain exploded.

"Yah. This is fun. Where to next?"

"Um." Either this was all a giant hallucination or...well she couldn't think of any "or". Except, or, this was all real.

"I do have a mission. I must find Isobel MacLeod...perhaps you know her, an old wise woman, my ancestor...she has disappeared." Meri hesitated. The birch tree and the dryad – could she speak aloud that eerie encounter?

"Mhmm," replied the Selkie brightly. "All creatures know Iseabail, our plant *sitheag*."

Plant fairy? And what the hell, she was talking to a seal-woman, a mythological selkie, with whom she'd just spent the morning surfing. "Um, and I think I met—"

"Pooh, thinking! Lovely, you humans overthink everything. Just swim and eat fish!"

Meri laughed. "A good rule for life."

"Of course! Now, your mission. I'll collect my seal-sisters and we'll attack with our long gleaming swords, and smash with our axes, and cast horrid spells!" The selkie bounced around on the sand, swinging imaginary lethal blades and crashing imaginary axes with such vivid movements even Meri blenched.

She stuttered, "I think I met a d-dryad. A woman in a birch tree. I think she said Isobel was 'taken' but I can't be sure."

"Oh dryads," said the selkie, in tones dripping scorn, "Such dreamers, always spouting ridiculous poetry and wanting to dance under the full moon. Can't get a word of sense from them." She sheathed her imaginary sword in her imaginary sword belt. "How did you call the dryad? They're getting harder and harder to wake, you know. Deaf, sleepy or lazy, who can tell?"

Meri blinked. "Call?" She rapidly reviewed what she'd done just before she saw the tree spirit. "Um. I pictured water, that's right, water everywhere, in the lochs and seas, in the ground, in the trees and plants, and in me. And I gifted a magical seal tooth to the loch."

Impulsively, the selkie embraced her. For a moment, Meri was cocooned in soft rubbery fish-scented fur, a soft, affectionate barking teasing her ear.

The selkie murmured, "I thought you was a seal-sister playing, and wondering why you didn't transform." She grinned. "Water *sìtheag*. Water fairy. It's been long and long, since one of those walked these islands. Not since legends became songs."

Meri barely registered the latter lines. The selkie's first words had arrested her, put her in handcuffs and slammed her hard against the wall. "Transform?" she whispered, small explosions of delight coursing in her veins. "Into a seal? And back?" She blinked rapidly, a long-held dream holding her in thrall.

The selkie laughed. "Maybe, lovely, maybe. Deep magic that, if you are not a seal-sister." She read Meri's crushed expression. "Never say never! I believed you a seal-sister myself, so perhaps you have just forgotten how to do it, coming from so far away."

"How did you know I was from far away? My Australian accent?"

The selkie rippled with a giggle that sounded like waves crashing. "I can smell the great Southern Ocean on you, the endless seas that lap the frozen continents where more of our seal sisters play."

"Oh wow," Meri replied, but the selkie was still talking, waving her arms, "I was born there, my love, a cub seal along the south west Victorian coast. My sisters and I came here to these islands and we have been playing here ever since. They needs us – needed us – to fight the English trying to steal these lands."

Gobsmacked was an understatement for Meri's tumult of emotion. So much to process.

Dreaming

Meri spoke aloud and waved her arms as she walked in the dream of the fun fair. "See all these creative questions, change them and the story changes again, magic mirrors at the fun fair, your first story distorted, sometimes ghastly, tall and wavery, short and squat, all driving you to insanity. Which is me? Which is the story, the fine, grand tale, that tells my truth?

"Pick one, pick one, but I'm lost in the mirror maze, all distortions equally me, me but not-me, can't find the way out.

"All good now, its like the roller coaster, a fun ride, round and round, hold on and scream to the end.

"So how do I find my way out of the magic mirror maze? Describe the reflections anyway, be in the maze, let one of them hold your hand and take you on a journey. There are as many stories and mad reflections – more – and you don't need to tell all of them, just let them hover and waver on the edge of your vison. Find the right one – maybe it is the tall smiling one? Me as I've never been in life! Or maybe the grimacing one."

Meri sat upright in bed on full alert.

What the hell?

CHAPTER FIVE
We meet some Seal sisters

"*What shall we do with a drunken sailor, what shall we do with a drunken sailor, what shall we do with a drunken sailor, earlie in the mornin'?*" My seal-sisters and I shouts the chorus together as we dives and dives again to roll and gambol in the luscious waves. "*Hoo ray and up she rises!*"

Selkies adore sea shanties! So jolly and rollicking, they exactly suits us.

"Fionn, sing us another!" Lenore barks, so I tumbles in a wave while I summons the next song, then begin the tune: "*So I tailed her my flipper and took her in tow."* My sisters shout, *"Way, aye, blow the man down!"* I yells, *"And yardarm to yardarm away we did go."* All of us, full barks and squeaks: *"Give me some time to blow the man down!"*

As we sing, we slide and slips, roll and tumbles, zoom and leaps – yum, fishy! Crunch, munch. Cool glide of salt water, crash and roar – mmm snap, swallow, more lovely wriggling fishies. Oh the slide of an ocean curl, the music of the sea, the tug and float and bounce.

And as we dives and swims, my seal-sisters and me, here we are too, in the battle.

There they are, the men, on the deck of the great ship, clad in armour of all kinds, chain mail, hauberks, big stomping boots over those feet and legs. Swords, cannons even. Ready to take our lands, with blood and sword if necessary, with deaths of their own, by the hundred, by the thousand, ten thousand.

I calls to my seal sisters, and my shark sisters, who are bound to their marine form, forever cruising the deep like shadows of doom. But sometimes we all need a shark sister.

The first spear comes like a...well, like a spear, straight into water. The men, hyped up on man-blood, war gods and war myths and stirring tales of manhood and never surrendering and glorious deaths, one of the men has spotted us seals, and thinks they will kill us for sport. To see the blood flow of another creature, they hungers for it, lusts for it...

Well, we'll show them hunger. They'll feel lust all right when my sisters and I are finished with them.

So my sisters and I, first we sings, in seal, some of our battle songs, our songs of oceans and continents shifting, of tides and moons and seasons. When the men are all holding spears and swords, leaning over the ship, stabbing into the breakers, my sisters and I transform.

We becomes human women above, with seal tails beneath, laughing, flicking great gobbets of ocean water up at the ship, calling insults, teasing and taunting, mocking, revealing a breast here, a curved cheek there.

The men go mad. They begins to jump over the side of the ship grasping hungry hands out to us; they fear naught for the magic, for when are men ever afraid of womenkind? Except for witches, of course, so they hunts those down and hangs or burns them all.

Or so they thinks.

As soon as a decent pod of armed men flail around in the water, my sisters and I transforms to seal and rakes their tender skin with our long, sharp claws; we bites them with our hard teeth, we sprays blood until our shark sisters came circling, circling.

Laughing, we leaves the blood-lusting men to their deserved fate and swim and walk out of the sea to shore.

As we get closer to the sand, we transforms our skins and body shape to human women. Immediately I feels the pang of loss: the siren of the sea, always calling me, faint or loud, yet always, always there like music in my blood, the music of my personal cells, bone deep, singing like a whale song, a beautiful howl of welcome and desire.

But that is all a mistake.

For now we becomes the hunted. The surviving men wants to take us to wife. They'd all heard the stories – hasn't everyone? Our claws and teeth excites them. The thought they could capture us, and hide our skins, to imprison we at their will, makes their own skins tingle with desire, with hunger and greed.

They wants a domestic selkie, her seal skin hidden, so she can never return to her true love, the great ocean. They care naught for our yearning, our sadness and loss. They imagines seal children, all in thrall to him, the man.

Ha ha ha. They don't know we have formed our own military order, that we ourselves have a sacred mission, to save our beautiful, lovely, complex seas.

Oh wait a minute – that ancient battle was long, long ago. Was, not is. A fun memory from universal seal-mind. Past blurs with present in the seal-dream.

Later – today? Yesterday? Next week? I swims with my friend Merilea and teach her sea shanties. *"Haul away, you rollin' king! Heave away, Haul away! Haul away, Oh hear me sing!"* we shout and scream, and together we surf the waves. She laughs and laughs, croaky and creaky at first, like she has almost forgotten how, then crazy-joyful as a selkie in the waves.

I smells the sea-smell in her. The sea calls and sings to her too. I wonder she does not transform to her true self. She would have so much fun!

CHAPTER SIX
Isobel imprisoned

I sobel bent once more to her desk, and her task, willing the spells to come. Every cell in her body screamed for her watery, hilly, island home, the big skies and waterbirds of her lovely Uist.

"MacLeod!" Isobel jumped. The harsh voice continued, "You are extremely lucky to have this chance, food and comfort—"

"—*good nursing care, even permitted to use your Talents...*" Isobel mentally echoed along with the woman. Maybe if she heard the lies enough times, she'd internalise them, begin to believe them herself.

She meekly bent her head to her work, hoping by this show of docility that the woman would seek another victim to berate.

No such luck.

The steely-eyed matron strode over, her huge bosom reaching Isobel before the rest of her battleship-shaped form. "MacLeod," she sneered, "You must work faster. We need the new spells by morning tea." Her sweaty face hovered closer. "Not good enough, MacLeod."

"Sorry Matron," said Isobel tonelessly. Anything for peace.

A mistake.

The woman's pudgy, beringed hand shot out. "Oh dear, whoops!" An inane giggle erupted as she spilt the inkpot all over Isobel's careful, delicate work. "That's no food for you, my love, until you've re-done the work to my satisfaction."

Isobel was careful not to meet the woman's gaze; yet not careful enough. She flicked a glance to the woman, and was transfixed by her tormentor's gloating, avid, lustful expression, enjoying her victim's distress.

Shocked soared through Isobel's cells. So. The Matron wasn't just hard, she absolutely enjoyed causing emotional pain. A tiny seed of rebellion lodged in Isobel's breast and sent out its first cotyledon, seeking fertile earth in which to grow.

Isobel bent her head in apparent submission but really to hide her hot flare of determination. She'd escape from here. She'd use everything she knew to flee. If she could just, somehow, summon Merilea...thank the old gods that this bully had no knowledge of her niece-relative.

You need Aged Care, they'd told her as they took her away. Risk of hollow bones, cracked ribs, as she lived alone, no-one to care, she'd be put in the recuperative centre. Instead, somehow she'd ended up here, in the magical workhouse. As if Isobel wasn't healthy as a sea eagle.

She'd been trying not to eat the terrible, drugged food. She was already skin and bone. She only ate enough to keep her brain active and her muscles functioning, and then battled against the fog creeping through her brain and the terrible lassitude weighing her limbs.

Without contact to earth, plants, trees, green living things, Isobel could feel her magic and strength dissipating, weakening. She stared down at the spilled ink – if only it was strong black tea, she'd lick it from the page, she was that desperate, even for such dishwater stuff they served the inhabitants here.

If she had water magic, then she could put a fingertip in the spillage and summon magical help. She suited the action to the thought; in her mind, she called and called to Meri.

Useless. Wrong magic.

She needed trees, plants, her feet in soil and sand. Here, she may as well be a drone like many of those that surrounded her.

How did all these folk bear the large open room? Where every scrape of a pen could be heard, every sigh, every muffled curse? Most seemed resigned

– were they so numb they'd lost all sensitivity and nuance?

Her mind slipped into another's vision – Merilea's? A similar large open office, a violent assault on the senses: the racket of chit-chatter, bitchy laughter, banging of drawers, scritch-scratching of pens, tapping keyboards, hissed arguments...and not just that. The weight of emotion in the room, emanating out, swamping her mind: the brooding resentments, petty jealousies, ambition bitter as lemon juice in the morning, the cliques and clans and exclusions; the sweaty desperation to belong, to impress, to climb the ladder; the negation and stagnation of people's own identity, submerged into this brown stagnant swamp of mediocrity...

Isobel wiped her brow with a trembling hand. She hadn't summoned Merilea a moment too soon. The woman's magic might be near dissipated if she'd spent years in that hostile environment.

Time for action, *sìtheag*! She peeked around. One door in and out. Two tiny windows near the ceiling, opened the merest crack. If she wanted to make a run for it, it would be a senior's run: hobbling, yet with an islander's strong, wiry endurance.

She had a last great effort in her.

How she longed for her home. Freedom. Blue skies, her native air, the sound of the sea like the sound of her own breathing, the sharp salt, seaweed smell, the cries of the wild birds...blessed silence. The heather, the machair studded with wildflowers, the deep green woodland.

Isobel squashed down the rush of terrible images of what they'd do to her if she tried to flee.

She edged her heavy chair out from the desk and bent down as though searching for a dropped pen. Her back spasmed a bit: not enough exercise! She breathed through it, lifted the desk a little, wrenched the ankle chain loop from the desk leg, and unfolded herself with a yelp of agony.

Just as she hauled herself to her feet, ready to run with all she had left out of the door and to freedom, the sound of an altercation arrested her.

The matron swept into the room, bashing a tiny wee lass, about twelve years old, with a huge straw broom. "Sweep that chimney or I'll set fire to your feet again!"

Isobel's gaze anchored on the little feet, blackened with soot – and yes, blisters.

Enough! When the lass came close, Isobel beckoned. The child startled as though afraid Isobel would hit her too. Isobel smiled, and crooned in Island Gaelic "Its fine, wee lassie. Come here, I want to talk to you." With eyes showing white all around, her thin body shaking, the child crept closer, no doubt drawn to the sound of her native speech; or perhaps simply the musical cadence of Gaelic, beloved by wild things, animals and nature spirits alike.

"Can ye find me a plant, with its roots still in soil, my love?" she said in Island Gaelic. Ah! Good guess! The wee lass nodded once, showing she was indeed an island lass somehow stolen away and forced to labour in this prison.

"Matron!" called one of the other workers. When Matron appeared, the worker stood up, and whispered in her ear, mouth prim and malevolent, gaze pinned on Isobel.

The matron's face purpled. Her chins shook.

Isobel whispered, "Pretend you picked up my pen and give it to me. Bonnie lass. Now, go quickly. Begone. Hide." The child faded away like a sunbeam, and quickly ducked behind a desk, creeping towards the door out of the matron's line of sight.

"What's this?" The matron marched over to Isobel's desk. "Interfering with the domestic staff?

That's Rule #13 broken." The smirk was a terrible thing to see. "No dinner either."

"I'll have no energy to do your work for you then." Isobel's heart beat a million miles an hour, smashing in her chest. Her vision went blurry. Her chest squeezed. All this for one mildly rebellious comment to the matron! Stiffen your spine, *sìtheag*. But her body was panicking, and her mind was screaming, be docile! Agree! She fought her fear. The child might bring a plant...

The matron's glare could have melted stone and should have been used for road surfacing, it was that hard and unforgiving.

Isobel forced the word past her pressed lips. "Please."

"You may have bread and water. Last warning!"

Isobel looked around her. Most folk had their heads down, patently absorbed in their work. Two women stared avidly. "Enjoying the show?" Isobel said, but in Gaelic.

"Speak like an Englishwoman, not a heathen!" the matron spat right in her face.

The hours crept by like ant steps. The child did not reappear. Perhaps she was being punished too.

Minute by minute, Isobel's magic died inside her. Magic was linked to joy, or even the fire of rage, something powerful and positive, not this death by increments that was working in an open-plan office under the tyranny of a volatile, intemperate, unpredictable bully.

Time to help herself. She just needed a plant connected to the earth.

"Try again," Fionn, her fabulous new selkie-friend said, her desperation-tinged, over-bright tone showing that her fragile patience was wearing thin. "Maybe I'll just blast you with my magic, get all my seal-sisters to blast you at once—" Delight rippled over the selkie's face. "Brilliant! Yes, let's do that!"

"Ah, no, let's try again," Meri said hastily, totally unsure of the effect of the unpredictable magic of a whole pod of selkies all blasting her with magic. "I *must* be a selkie, it's the only thing that makes sense. I've just forgotten how to change...all those years trying so hard to fit into the mundane world has withered my natural powers."

"Alright, one more time," Fionn agreed cheerfully, then suddenly whirled, scooped up Meri before she knew what was happening, and threw her off the rock platform into the wild, heaving, freezing, smashing, deadly sea.

"Arghhhhh!" Meri screamed, before seawater engulfed her face. The tides tumbled her over and over in the huge breakers; a massive wave picked her up high, her entire torso hanging out of the water for five long seconds; all Meri could see was the lethal, wave-wet rocky cliff speeding closer and closer, inevitable as a train wreck...

A strong, smooth seal body flipped her over. Disaster averted in the nick of time. Fionn and two other seals dragged her further out to sea, then carried her in an eddy back to the rock shelf, where more selkie hands pulled her to safety.

Meri hardly knew whether to cry, scream at her friend, laugh hysterically or swear, and discovered she was doing them all simultaneously.

Rubbery seal flippers patted her awkwardly; selkie-human hands smoothed her cheeks and hair. Multiple round brown eyes stared at her, frustration and puzzlement in every gaze.

"Bless my barnacles, you can't be a selkie, my love," said Orla, the old spotted seal. "One would imagine you would have changed then."

New desperation surged in Meri's belly, as agitated as the heaving seas below the platform. "I must be! I *am*! I've just forgotten. I need more time."

But more than one seal face bristled sympathetic whiskers and blinked long-lashed eyes. Fionn gave her a jolly smile. "Not to worry, Meri, we'll get there."

But despair tickled with grey fingers in Meri's mind. Maybe she'd lost her special magic forever, by ignoring and denying it her whole life. Now, she wondered why she'd complied with social demands for so many decades. How she yearned to be able to transform into a seal and swim with her sisters! It might be the only way she could save Isobel.

Back at the Hobgoblin Hotel, Donald had bidden her wait before calling any mainland authorities. "You risk making it all worse," he'd growled. "If she needs aid, it will be island help that one needs." *Island*, as in *magical*, Meri surmised.

Guilt clawed in her belly. The flora *sìtheag* had been fine before Meri decided to seek her out. Had she inadvertently triggered the events which led to her ancestor's possible capture? The horrible idea firmed her determination. She would transform, she would! And then she and her seal-sisters would search for Isobel and rescue her.

Meri swam and bodysurfed with the selkies for another dangerous and delightful hour, and at last lay completely exhausted, warming herself on the rock shelf with her seal friends.

They all lay around, barking and grunting happily. Orla, the old spotted selkie-seal said, "By the way, someone is calling you."

Meri sat up. "Calling me? Who?" She gazed around wildly. "I can't hear anything."

The selkie shrugged. "Old. Old magic. Not water magic, plant magic. The message was very faint. I almost forgot."

"*Isobel!* Where is she?" Meri asked eagerly.

The selkie flopped over, not answering, while Meri fidgeted. Then the old seal croaked, "You'll have to ask a Dryad now, but getting one of those stayabeds to pay attention is more than I have patience for! We selkies love action, and singing, and swimming, and eating fish; those girls droop and drape around inside their trees, being beautiful and murmuring plaintive poems about groundwater and springs, sap and springtime."

A dryad? Meri had a flash of the woman in the tree. "How do I call the dryad?" She met many pairs of interested brown eyes. "I'll return to where I saw the dryad first, near Isobel's cottage. She manifested near an ancient birch tree – I think that must be hers."

The selkies all barked encouragement. "Action!" enthused Ocena, a younger dark grey seal, flapping her arms close to her body like flippers. "You'll always feel better when you move and act. Too much thinking gets you nowhere."

Meri grinned as she waved goodbye. She loved the selkies' "Embrace the moment! Act first, think later" philosophy. It made her feel so alive, tingling all over with glee and hope.

Not being able to transform – yet – Meri rubbed the remaining water from her face and skin, grabbed her clothes from behind the dune and hastily tugged them on.

It was the noise that alerted her first. Banging. Loud voices. The roar of a chainsaw. And a kind of silent screaming in her brain. Meri sprinted around the curve of the woodland track on swim-rubbery legs – and stopped, aghast.

A huddle of high-vis clad men, leaning on a work truck, one revving the chainsaw, obscured her vision of the dryad tree.

"Act first!" she scolded herself. "Act now. Isobel's rescue might depend on it." Out loud, she shouted, "No!" as powerfully as she could, and raced on her arthritic knees to the men.

Faces turned towards her – and she knew one of those faces, had distrusted and feared it. Her instincts had been right all along.

She said, her tone dripping with disgust, "Murdo MacIver!" She marched forward, hands on hips, taking time to rake Murdo and each of his companions with her most ferocious gaze. "What on earth are you doing with Isobel MacLeod's prized tree?"

Murdo looked startled, then furious, then stubborn. His head jerked back, lips curling. He waved a hoary hand with a faux-airy gesture. "It's a wilding. An old, trespassing, wilding birch. Needs to be cleaned up."

Meri thought fast. Decades of working in bureaucratic government offices might have their uses after all. She stood straight, summoned all the words she'd made dance and sing over all the years, and said, "I am Isobel MacLeod's relative." She looked at the chainsaw man, and snapped, "Turn that thing off!"

The man jumped and obeyed. Blessed silence.

"This is Isobel MacLeod's property and this tree is on her land."

"It's on public land," Murdo growled. His terrible black frown was turning her knees to jelly, eroding her spine, but she pushed her fear down. Meri channelled a bureaucratic, highly offended government minister, donning her personality and demeanour like a glamour.

She cut Murdo off. She flapped her fingers in a summoning gesture. "Paperwork?" She raised scornful brows. "Show me this is on public land. Show me your authority for cutting this tree down."

She whipped around to one of the high vis men, put on her most precise educated voice. "Get away from that tree until I see signed, official confirmation for its removal. And then, you will need to wait until the appeal period is over, generally twelve weeks, I assume?" she added, inventing wildly. As long as it sounded authoritative.

Murdo laughed. "Get over yourself, Aussie interloper. What would you know—"

She rounded on him, cutting him off, fury sparking. *Careful.* Don't let your magic show. She made her voice clear and firm. "Get. Away. From. Isobel's. Land. Now."

Just then, a figure alighted from the driver's side of the truck.

Meri's heart plummeted. She felt like such a fool. Dolina from the cafe's lovely face smiled at her, and her beautiful Gaelic-accented voice reproved her. "Whit would ye know aboot our doings, lass? Ye are a good woman for protecting your relative, but she asked us to remove this wee tree." She smiled at Chainsaw Man. "Let's get yon saw goin' again and let we be done with all this fuss."

Dolina's voice was so soothing, Meri almost found herself nodding along. She had to focus not to let herself be charmed and persuaded. A thought flitted: did Dolina have her own magic?

She pressed her lips together, firmed her jaw and marched to the tree. "No, you will not. You will show me paperwork. And I will have the time needed for an appeal."

Murdo said, "Dolina?" Dolina made a gesture, and her hands were filled with official-looking papers.

"No," Meri said. Betrayal fluttered in her heart like a trapped moth with tarnished wings. She'd *liked* Dolina. And Murdo.

Dolina said, in her musical voice, "Isobel has had the papers for months. She has already used the appeal time. We even gave her an extra month, but as we have had no response…" She smiled. Like every bully smile Meri had ever seen. No, the bullies would *not* win this battle. She didn't know anything about dryads – if they chopped down her tree, would she die?

An idea froze her blood. What if the birch was some kind of portal? And removing it would trap Isobel?

Meri's brain jumped and short-circuited. There must be something... Then she had it. "Isobel told me this tree is on the International Register of Significant Trees. That totally overrules any pathetic local ordinance you might have there." She smiled as falsely as Murdo and Dolina. "It's known locally as a Fairy Tree. It's also registered with the International Society of Folklore and Fairytales."

Chainsaw Man turned his machine off again. His face had paled so severely Meri wondered if he would faint. Ha! A superstitious local. She pushed her advantage and said directly to him, her tone savage, "Aye. If you so much as nick this tree, it's not the bureaucracies you have to worry about. The *sìtheanach* will be coming for you, in your dreams and on every path you walk."

The man blanched, shook his head, backed away. He opened the truck and, as carefully as if it were a baby, placed the chainsaw on the back seat. "I'll nae be doing aught agin' the Folk," he muttered, and squeezed himself into the truck alongside his power tool. The two other men looked at Meri, wide-eyed, and quickly followed suit.

Murdo glowered. She didn't permit herself even a small smirk but gave him a full glare in response. He said, voice low, "I'm surprised you had it in you. However, ye will nae be here every minute of every day, will ye now, lass?" His tone was laced with malice.

He did smirk when he saw her terrified reaction, turned his back and alighted the work truck. Dolina patted her arm, smiled fondly as though they hadn't just been at loggerheads, got into the driver's seat and the whole party roared off with a spray of churned up peat fragments.

Meri's whole body shook in reaction. Her knees suddenly gave way and she plonked down under the tree. "Oh, oh, oh!" she said aloud. "You are fine, you are fine..." A few tears sprouted but she wiped them away with a hasty hand. "You are *fine*."

She patted the glowing pale bark. "And you are fine too, pretty tree, at least for now."

And then the air shimmered, and there she was. The beautiful, drooping, drapery-clad dryad. The dryad sat down next to Meri and placed her chin on one long, elegant hand. "You may have one wish, sweet saviour," she said.

"Oh, goddesses and gremlins, this is like the fairy-tales, isn't it? I must get my one wish right or all is lost." Meri scrunched her face up. "I am desperate to help Isobel – but I guess I should be wishing those men don't come back to chop your lovely tree down."

"Mmm," murmured the dryad, rather infuriat-ingly. She tilted her face up to Meri's. "Sea magic," she said. "Seashells, pretty seashells, floaty green seaweed, in the ocean deeps."

Meri waited. "That was a lovely poem, thank you," she said at last. Why hadn't Fionn and the other selkies told her how to interact with a dryad? Obeying a sudden mad impulse, based on reading thousands of fairytales, she burst into song. "Heave ho, and up she rises, earlie in the morn-in'!"

The dryad rolled her eyes. "You've been spending time with selkies," the creature said in tones of strong disapproval. "Rowdy, fish-smelling things."

Meri tried again, amending the lyrics to suit her situation. "Where-air-air is Iso-bel? Where-air-air is she? Is she with the clouds above? Or flying with a dove? Oh where-air-air can she be?"

The dryad laughed and clapped in delight. "Oooh pretty!" she crooned. "Isobel-elle-elle has been snatched oh la! From her cottage in the woods, oh la! Isobel-elle-elle is in the magi-cal work-house, ooh ah, ooh ah oh!"

"How do I find it?" Meri asked quickly. "Can you tell me the way?"

The dryad made a few faces, then yawned and replied petulantly, "I'm bored with this now," glimmered, wavered, and she was gone.

Meri leaped to her feet. "Hey!" she shouted, whacking the slender tree trunk with her palm. "Hey! What about my wish?"

And then, the Hobgoblin Hotel host, Donald MacNeil, emerged from the edge of woodlands, regarding her with a quizzical smile. Oh, by all the ancient fairy folk, what had he seen? What had he heard? He brandished his basket of fungi at her as though in explanation, so she nodded dumbly, poleaxed with delayed shock.

Then the man winked. WTF? Meri gazed after him narrow-eyed as he meandered back to his hotel. She had no doubt that man knew far more than he was letting on.

The dryad didn't reappear. She'd best go and consult with the selkies once more. At least they'd advocate action of some kind!

Fionn declared, full of enthusiasm, "Shall I come with you, bring my weapons, find out where Isobel is, and we can do a smash and grab of your old woman?"

"Yes! Would you?" Meri beamed.

The selkie scratched her legs where her sleek tail had been. "It's more fun if I bring my sisters. There might even be selkie-sisters imprisoned there, leaked of their magic in weird bloodletting rituals. I've heard of such things." For a moment, the selkie's normally sunny expression darkened. "I won't have it! I won't have seal-sisters hunted and abused." She nodded vigorously. "It's time for – *the return of the selkies!*"

Infected by the selkie's victory fist pump, Meri gave a rousing cheer. They shouted together:

"The Return of the Selkies!"

CHAPTER SEVEN
Puffin chat and Whale song

"Bring me a plant in soil, wee one." Isobel kept the request alive in her mind; but eventually, hope began to flicker and fade. Just as she began to think dispiritedly, "Oh well, this magical workhouse isn't so bad, every day at two pm I can see the sun there in the tiny window across the room, and really my colleagues are quite nice, I'm sure they burst into whispers and laughter about something unrelated when I'm marched in every morning; just as she began to talk to the others, to try to make friends, to let the grinding boredom and routine wither her soul worse than any magic manacle could do; just

when she began to say "yes matron" and mean it,
just when she resolved to "make the best of it",
the child shuffled forward to her desk, snuck a
look around, and shoved a bundle of rags at her.

Terrified, the child shook all over, pointing to
Isobel's water glass. The glass was filled every
three hours; Isobel husbanded it carefully, tim-
ing her sips.

But now, she raised a brow, and handed the
glass to the child, who took great thirsty gulps.
As Isobel's water vanished, the child's skin's began to plump out, her cheek bloom with a rosy
sheen, her eyes grow sparkle. "Thank ye," the
child whispered in forbidden Scots Gaelic. "I
left a little water for the plant; ye mun water the
poor thing.'

"Matron!" Shrieked a colleague. "The child is speaking Gaelic to the hag."

The Hag? That's what's they all called her, *The Hag*?

Quick, thought Isobel, no time for that. "Bide quiet, child, and together we'll get out of here," she whispered. "Quick now, face down, don't show them you've had water." The child nodded, and slid away in her shuffling walk, face down, shoulders hunched against insult and abuse.

Hurry. Hide this thing, whatever the wee lass has brought her.

"Matron!" screamed her colleague, standing up and staring to see what Isobel was doing. More erstwhile friends stood and hollered, "Matron! Matron, the child spoke to the Hag-witch."

Without looking, her fingers felt under the rags. *Empty*. No! Her body broke into a fear-sweat as a terrible surety flitted in her mind. Betrayal tasted sour on her tongue.

This was nothing but a trick.

The matron burst in, blowing steam and sneering. Everyone laughed, cat-calling and mocking. Isobel felt her last hope desiccate and die.

"And," added one colleague whom Isobel had tried to befriend, listening to long boring stories about her entire extended family and all their illnesses, "the child drank most of her water too!" Three colleagues positively screamed with laughter and fell about in what Isobel considered unnecessary hysterics.

"No matter," the Matron sneered. "Servant can work another three hours, if she is full of water, until she dries out again."

The child shuffled backwards until she banged against a wall, where she cowered, her arm over her head.

Isobel watched, outraged. By what harm had the Matron persuaded the child to speak against her? Concern simmered, for she could have sworn the child hated and feared the terrible Matron. And that phrase the Matron used, "until she is dried out again" ...hmm. It sparked a notion in Isobel's brain.

As she watched the huddled, shaking form, as though aware of Isobel's scrutiny, the child suddenly removed her arm and met Isobel's gaze with eyes resolute and glittering, and raised one filthy finger to her lips. Shh. The moment passed, and the child resumed greeting softly and shaking in her corner.

Matron loomed like a black tower, filled with menace, over Isobel's desk. "Give me that! She snatched the bundle away and tossed it on the floor. "There is no escape. You must work your way in the world, in the way specified in this magical workhouse. If you behave, after sufficient years of good behaviour, you might get to choose another role – or gain promotion. This is life; lose your silly fancies. To Work!"

She faced the room. "All of you! To Work!"

"Work, work, work," They all echoed obediently.

It was that very evening in the big workroom, Isobel made to work a longer shift "to make up for the work you missed," as most of the others headed off for their meagre dinner, that the child appeared once more. Isobel's heart leaped, then squeezed, the recent betrayal still stinging like a scorpion's bite.

But she gave the child her water once more. This time the sprite sipped only twice, breathed "thank you, plant-witch-mother" in Scots Gaelic, reached under her ragged woollen top, pulled something out and shoved another small wrapped bundle in Isobel's lap.

Isobel's hands rested on the bundle. The child vigorously applied her broom to sweeping. Isobel regarded the room. In the bustle of departure for the day, had no one witnessed this interaction? She trusted nobody now.

Her hands rested lightly on the bundle, then her fingers crept beneath the dirty rags, and touched...a tiny leaf. Bark. A short, twisted truck...and soil.

Isobel called her power. For a moment that familiar fizz in her veins, her pulses igniting—

Then instead of a fizz, a fizzle. A sort of weak signal, a tiny pull.

Her inner self, her power was far away. Wounded. Damaged.

This must be how mundanes feel. How utterly tragic. She should free all of these people here, not just herself.

Selkies prepare for battle

Meri sat on the rock platform, the inaccessible, impossible shelf jutting out from the cliff into the foaming waves, fresh salt air tingling in her nostrils. She sat very close to her new friend Fionn, the selkie. Around them, in attitudes of utter relaxation, lay seals: spotted harbour seals, sleek grey seals, fur seals, sea lions and even a couple of elephant seals. Some of them rolled over lazily in the sun. Others rose up onto their flippers and gyrated to the edge of the shelf, throwing themselves into the sea with suddenly smooth, graceful, athletic speed. And others still had assumed human form, and sat in relaxed, sprawling attitudes in a vague circle.

Meri eyed them with mingled excitement, wonder and trepidation. Most looked as relaxed as an Aussie surfer, but she could see their teeth and claws up close and personal.

"Ho, a fight!" said Orla, the older, grey-spotted harbour seal – or at least she had been a few minutes before. Now she was an older woman, as fit and muscular as the other selkies, with silver hair streaked with dark grey and the kind, lit-up eyes of all the selkies.

A few selkies honked in united enthusiasm and surrounding seals barked with them. The selkies all called out, voices tumbling over each other, as joyfully and riotously as they surfed the ocean swells. "Weapons!" "Magic!"

A grey seal with markings around its eyes wriggled and banged its tail and transformed into an older human woman wearing spectacles. "Fionn, dear, do supply us with details, so we don't just rush off and fight anyone in our way."

The seals thumped their tails and the selkies applauded. "Yes, bonza, mate!" Meri stared. Surely that was an Australian fur seal? "Brilliant! Details! Who'd a' thought of that? Clever Orla!"

Meri shot the selkie a suspicious glance, but she appeared to be perfectly in earnest. A bubble of laughter exploded inside Meri. Something of their joy of life began to transfer to her own blood, helped by the fabulous body surf she'd just experienced with the pod.

Fionn waved her arms and barked a little. "Our seal-sister here—" The selkies all applauded and barked in hooting sounds again. A surge of strong emotion welled up in Meri; she began to laugh, and realised she had not felt so welcome, so entertained, so belonging, as she did right now with her seal-sisters.

Fionn said, "The Plant Faerie. She's been taken to the magical workhouse—"

Now groans of horror echoed around the rock shelf. Meri could only admire: seals and selkies certainly knew how to groan, throwing themselves into the full expression of groaning, putting all their lung capacity and torso strength into it, like an opera of double bass and cello and the ocean booming from a blowhole. The rock shelf had resounded with groans and moans for a good five minutes, then Fionn resumed her tale.

"The dryad told Meri—"

She waited while the selkies made dismissive and derisory comments about dryads. Meri giggled. It was impossible to feel gloomy or doomy with this insouciant mob of seals and selkies. All her doomy, gloomy weights inside her were dissolving, mellowing...she remembered that life can be a joy, full of sparkle and dazzle, and that facing troubles with friends made burdens so much lighter... Friends...she'd forgotten how to make them and keep them, until now.

Friends. She smiled and hugged the sizzle of joy into her heart.

Fionn rapidly outlined the dryad's complex message about the magical workhouse.

A fat old selkie who'd been lying flat-backed and spreadeagled, soaking up the sun's gentle warmth, rolled over and barked, "Magical workhouse? That infernal team will be draining her magic. We must hurry."

Meri wasn't sure if that selkie knew how to hurry, but she was willing to be surprised.

"How will we find the workhouse?" asked the be-spectacled one, Wenda.

The older one hauled herself to a sitting position. "I've heard the whales sing that it exists in no time and every time."

The selkies were silent, emanating respect. Meri looked around the circle. Apparently whales were held in high esteem.

The old selkie looked Meri. "The whales live for eons. They know the secrets of the sea, for all the sea creatures tell them. They sing to each other of oceans and time, of icebergs and ships with harpoons, and warm seas full of plankton, and the trails of the stars." She smiled bashfully. "It takes a long time to learn whale song; it's very different from the song of seal-sisters."

The selkies and seals all murmured in a chorus of awe and approval.

Suddenly a selkie bounced up onto her feet with an athletic leap. "I'll call the puffin-crew. They'll know stories too." The selkie whistled a complicated tune underlaid by a beat of gentle grunting and chirping.

Australian Meri absolutely held her breath as first one, then a small flock of puffins landed on the shelf, eyeing the seals with caution. A horrid idea pulsed: did seals *eat* puffins? She'd never seen the adorable creatures, ever, as they did not come to Australian shores. To Meri's delighted, fond gaze, the puffins were like cute little comedians, with a comical face, huge orange beak, waddling walk, and emitting the same the chirping, grunting sound of the selkie. Wonder filled her.

Some of the seals stirred, staring at the puffins. The sprightly selkie admonished them, "No, you all! These lovelies are no snack for you today." She made shooing gestures, striding to the edge of the platform and huddling the puffins in a little chirping group.

The selkie had a long grunting, clicking, murmuring chat with them, and came back. "They will tell the whales where we are going. And now, here's how we find the workhouse."

She then reverted to seal language, a seal-song beyond Meri's powers to follow. It hardly mattered. Meri was totally in thrall to the selkies and seals. She *knew* they were mistaken, and she was indeed a seal-sister who had forgotten her powers, had forgotten how to be fully a seal, how to transform into a human with the knowledge how to morph back into a seal.

All she had remaining was that constant, background yearning for the sea; sometimes a mere

faint tickle; sometimes a craving so loud, so fran-
tic and urgent that as she got older with a little
more cash in the bank, she was finally able to just
book a weekend hotel by one of Victoria's stunning surf beaches and go swimming morning and
night until she could return to her workaday life,
having fully immersed in the ocean and restored
once more. It never left her, that craving; now
she wondered why she had let her husband always
dictate where they lived, deep inland, far from
even a stray sea breeze bringing olfactory news of
the great ocean.

But most of her life, how she had suffered –
she assumed everyone felt this way, and only the
wealthy could indulge themselves with a beach
house; but now, she had begun to realise, in
her fifties and sixties, that not everyone was

bored with administrivia; not everyone hated the mind-numbing nature of cleaning; not everyone wanted to throw themselves into any body of water they saw, and constantly, always, yearned for the sea.

The puffin-speaker kissed the puffins' cute beaks, each and every one, then waved them off into the sky. Meri thought she'd love to kiss those sweet puffin faces herself.

"Weapons!" called Fionn. All the selkies cheered and barked. They all heaved themselves upright and strode and waddled into the cave from which the rock shelf depended.

Meri found herself in a red and gold glowing wonderland, rife with stalactites and stalagmites, twisted into magical shapes, like hunched dwarves, and huge rock giants, and grinning witches...for all she knew, they'd turn out to be alive too.

The selkies began pulling long gleaming swords from rock shelves; shields, maces, spiky things, armour. Chatting, joking and singing snatches of battle songs and rousing sea shanties, they helped each other pull on leather iron-studded armour, plait their long hair into crowns, and some of the younger selkies tugged short soft leather boots onto their feet, with squeals of horror. Other seals rejected any footwear.

"No boots?" said Meri.

"No lovely, most of we fight barefoot," Ocena said.

"Do the boots hurt?" asked Meri.

"Aye, a little, but it's more because we hate them. We like sand underfoot, seawater flowing between our toes. Our feet are very sensitive, are not yours?"

Meri thought about it. "Well yes, my feet are very misshapen now, from wearing the wrong shoes most of my life."

Fionn laughed merrily. "All shoes are the wrong shoes, my love."

And then, they went to fight.

A strange haunting music woke Isobel; she held it tight in her core, but it fled, rudely shattered as the wooden door to her rough attic sprang wide.

"You must work to eat," instructed the Matron. "And work if you wish to sleep, wear clothes, and even, if you are very diligent, have a short break outside." The door slammed as she left on her rounds of torment.

Isobel was already failing. Without magic to sustain her, without her beloved harsh, wild landscape and its flora, without the music of seabirds and the song of the ocean, she was fading. Try as she might, her magical work, her output deteriorated.

Already, she'd gone from sleeping in a comfortable bed, she realised now, in her own small room in the workhouse, to a less comfortable bed in a mouldy, ramshackle room; and thence, as her work grew less valued, to a narrow iron bed in a long dormitory, kept awake by her colleagues' snores and moans, and finally, to a heap of rags in a hot, airless corner of a forgotten attic, far from soil and plants, as far from the person she had been as it was possible to get.

She hoped. Surely it couldn't get worse.

And the food! The first to lessen in quality was the fresh fruit and vegetables. In the beginning – how much time had elapsed? She'd eaten greens bursting with flavour and vitamins, fruit in season, peaches, raspberries, grapes, dripping with juice, and now? Fewer fresh fruits and vegetables, often frozen, then rehydrated peas and mashed potatoes with toxic, chemical flavour, small glasses of rehydrated orange juice.

Her concentration suffered, made worse by the perpetual bullying and sniping by her colleagues.

She was awash in misery. She'd almost totally lost hope.

She uncovered the plant given by the little skivvie, for the thousandth time. Try as she might, she could raise no more than a buzz of magic from the poor thing, bonsaied almost to a stupor.

Well she knew how that felt, as though her mind and limbs were bound with wire, twisted out shape for the edification of a mad collector. Isobel the bonsaied fae.

She held the plant, her fingers touching the tiny scrape of soil. Each day she saved a spoonful of water from her meagre allowance, to keep this poor, deprived plant alive. "Meri," she called. "Meri. Blood of my blood, bone of my bone."

And then she'd think better of it – for she did
not want Meri caught up in this hellish life, working all day for food and a place to sleep, which
she would be if she was caught; Isobel hadn't
found her relative's magic, yet she could feel the
woman's power: she radiated with it. And if Matron found Meri, she would put Meri through
terrible tests until, under pressure, her Talent was
revealed – or broken forever.

No. Despising herself for her moment of weak-
ness, Isobel hid the plant again and vowed she
would not try to call Meri again to aid her. Better Meri found another magical destiny guide.
Or, perhaps, become one herself unaided, for the
landscape itself would teach her.

The selkies were camped in a sea cave, halfway there according to Orla. Most of the selkies had swum, while Fionn and Meri transported all the weapons. Fionn had been jumpy and excited riding in the car, entertaining Meri with her startled exclamations and hilarious observations.

"I should make you learn to drive as revenge," Meri said mock-seriously, and then could have bitten her tongue out. Indeed, Fionn spent the rest of the journey begging her to do just that.

They'd eaten a fishy supper, then all slept in a tangle of seal-bodies.

Meri tossed and turned, half-excited by the forthcoming battle, awakened from her slumbers by a faint call: Isobel, she thought, the old woman's voice in her mind sounding far away, reedy and thin, in extremis. "Hold on!" she thought back. "The Selkies are coming!"

A snatch of a dream lingered then flashed away, embedded in an eerie, haunting, echoey song.

Dreaming

She flowed through the great ocean, her calf by her side. After a long swim from Antarctica, she and her calf rested in the warmer harbour of Portland, Australia. When she threw herself high in the air, she spied the crowds of humans running, running towards the beach, some with giant black tubes in their arms, others with small oblongs, held before their faces. The great whale rolled in the warm water, lazily waving a fin at the humans.

Stupid things. They didn't know how to communicate with anything, not even the over-friendly, garrulous dolphin-kin.

She hardly knew why they bothered to watch them. She and her calf rolled around for a while, swimming close to the harbour, listening to the cheers and exclamations – but not too close, not spear- or harpoon-close; she remembered what happened to Uncle. A bloody mess that was.

She nudged her calf. Show's over. Time to go. As she began the long swim north up the eastern Australian coastline, she began the new whale-song: a song of calving and babies, of plankton, and old friends in warmer seas.

The Old One had gone now, back to be part of the great ocean once more, and now she would continue the new whale-song for all the pods in this stretch of the ocean. She'd weave a new melody, the layers of whale-song knitting and tumbling around each other, the same and yet never quite the same, like waves in the sea...and then other whales would sing with her, swimming on the same journey, weaving in new navigation notes and warnings of harpoon ships, and stories of new calves and lost calves, and rich plankton, sunrises and sunsets, and songs of the moon and stars shining on their sea...the other whales would sing too, and weave in their own heart-songs and melodies, and then together they'd sing of the waves and the fish, of green and blue distance, of saltwater and salt air, of journeys and oceans. And eventually all of the whales in all the oceans on all the earth would sing this same song, for this year.

The whale songs were always begun in the great southern oceans.

And she began the first notes of her melodic, minor key, conversation with the universe.

"Meri! Meri! Wake up!"

She awoke with a jerk. Blinking, she gazed around her, trying to orientate herself. Oh. She was standing in the selkie cave.

All the selkies were staring at her in wonder and amazement: a great circle of soft brown eyes. Some stood tall, their hands on weapons. Others kneeled, gazing at her. A few still lay in their seal-furs, heads turned towards her.

Meri rubbed her arms, still feeling the balm of ocean water lapping on her skin. She ran her tongue around her mouth, which tasted weirdly of plankton. What? How did she know how plankton even tasted— Sensation rushed in her mind. The tail end of a most incredible dream lingered momentarily, then vanished in a snap of synaptic electricity.

She wanted to describe her dream to Fionn, if only she could remember; as she spoke, the selkies all came to their feet, wide-eyed. Meri realised she wasn't speaking words, but singing; without volition or effort, what issued from her mouth was a song. An eerie, unearthly, beautiful crooning song that somehow spake of her own heart's heart.

She tried to cling, to the sea-song, to the peace flooding her, the wonder, but normal thoughts rushed into her brain like dirty floodwater over a flower garden.

The song was gone. There was only Meri.

"What the hell, sister?" exclaimed Fionn.

"Ready, seal-sister, ocean friend?" Fionn called, grinning and waving two enormous swords in a complicated dance. All the Selkies pulled out their swords with a sound of swooping steel, and began to dance out on the sand in a complicat-ed, beautiful formation, singing a complex seal battle song full of grunting and bellowing and roars. Sunlight gleamed on swords, glinted from sharp daggers, and fled from spiky maces and swooping axes. They flung their arms high, bellowing; they crouched low and wriggled in a line then jumped high and wide again. They clashed weapons, linked arms and spun each other in wild circles.

Meri's heart lifted with her seal-sisters. Both ferocity and joy soared in her blood. "I'm alive! I'm alive!" she cried. "How glorious to be here, with my seal-sisters, in this mad dance."

Fionn swept forward and pulled her into the dance, and Meri was whirling, ducking weapons as they slashed through the air, stomping and barking and bellowing with them all. It was sort of like being at a footy match when your team has come from behind and snatches an epic victory. The sense of blending with a group, of dancing and laughing together. The sort of feeling where you spontaneously hug strangers for the unbridled victory exploding in your veins.

"Here," said Fionn. "Drink this. Eat this." And Meri drank a salty, seaweedy concoction that seemed to buzz through her veins, lending her – or reminding her – of her power and strength.

A sort of huge sensation filled her a moment; like she wanted to explode out of the ocean in a burst of energy, water rushing from her blubber...

No, that was the dream! She laughed, and stepped into the huddling, moving, shoving, laughing group, reminiscent of seals swimming over and around each other, except on land.

CHAPTER EIGHT
The Return of the Selkies

"We are going to transport via the Callanish Fairy Ring," Fionn explained. She added, after tossing a small, raw fish into her mouth and chewing with pleasure, "We need your magic."

Meri stood poleaxed. "But Fionn," she whispered urgently, "There's a slight prob—"

"Flap my flippers, it's off to the Fairy Ring!" called Orla. "The Fairy Ring!" echoed Ocena.

"Whoo hoo!" said Fionn, beaming. "Haven't had a fight in two hundred years."

Meri tried, and failed, to grab Fionn's forearm. "Fionn, I must expl—"

"*En garde*!" Fionn whipped out her sword and play-slashed it around Meri. At least she hoped it was play-slashing. The selkies appeared rather formidable in their training drills.

That evening, the group swam and drove to the island of Lewis, *Eilean Leòdhais*, where they stayed at an older selkie's sweet cottage, rented out as a holiday let.

"My husband caught me many years ago, when the world, and I, were young," she told Meri as they drank floral whisky. "He hid my skin. I bore him seven strong daughters and a son, and when he died, I found my skin, carefully preserved and wrapped, with a note inside thanking me for all my years of wifely devotion. He also left me this cottage and a very comfortable independence." She sipped her whisky. "Now, my dear, I seldom transform, I just put on my wetsuit!"

Meri laughed with her, but the old selkie saw the question in Meri's eyes. She patted Meri's hand with her own hand, now knobbly and spotted with arthritis and age. "When the crescent moon is shining on the seas, and the aurora dances, then my dear, then I transform and bathe in the beautiful ocean. I loop the loop and surf the breakers and feel gratitude for all life has given me."

Meri was a bit too choked up to reply.

"Yes, my dear, even my human existence. For the love of a good man is a treasure indeed." Her eyes lit with a mischievous smile. "When I say love, I refer also to physical love, of course."

Meri snorted a laugh and choked on her whisky. The old selkie beamed. A dreamy expression softened her face. "Though I do remember, when I was a seal maiden, a selkie, and met a fine young bull, oh now that is something to be experienced!"

Meri quickly swallowed another mouthful, bending her face over her glass to hide her blush. Seal sex! Her whole body twanged at the thought.

Perhaps as a result of the old selkie's confidences, and her grateful, open, humorous view of what life had brought, or maybe just the thousand remarkable things that had happened to Meri once she set foot on the lands of her ancestors, she felt restless. Her blood jumped and danced. Her skin tingled. Her muscles bounced with energy, craving movement.

It was late. Even the summer sun had retired, leaving just its golden gloaming glow over the landscape. The aurora was dancing and swirling blue and green and purple in the night sky.

She stepped out and inhaled the glorious, sweet, cool, salt-tinged air. Shadows moved in the landscape, as though magical things were abroad. Meri hardly cared. She felt magical herself, part of the mystery and majesty of her native soil and air.

As she came to a small copse of Scots Pine trees, she was hardly surprised when a shadow quivered around the creviced trunks and her dryad-friend stepped into her path.

The dryad looked her up and down and said in a sweet voice like rain in leaves, "I am visiting a friend's tree." The creature preened. "The tree had a red and orange fire devil living in it, but with the help of the lovely rains, we chased it away. Lot of sad trees infested with red and orange fire devils in them where you lived before. I can smell them on your skin."

Meri echoed, blinking, "Where I come from."

The dryad said, twirling in the gloaming, "You come from *here*."

Meri huffed a breath. "I suppose there's no point in wishing to avoid silliness and talking at cross-purposes tonight?"

"You may have your owed wish. I will open the gate tonight," the dryad replied, chin elevated haughtily. "While the sky dances."

"The gate?" Meri, a well-read fantasy reader (in addition to romance and crime) zinged with caution. Magical gates were always part of an adventure, but you had to be careful.

"Ah...the sel – *my friends*," she said in a quick save, remembering in time the dryad's disdainful views on selkies, "Are all asleep." A wave of vision washed over her. The portal opening. The magical workhouse. And her with no idea, none, what to do, how to find Isobel. "What can I do, alone? I can't even find my magic very often, I certainly can't manage to transform, try as I might..." Her voice rang with her own frustration.

She'd hesitated too long. The dryad rolled her eyes like an exasperated teenager, and vanished.

Meri tapped the fissured bark gently. "Hello? Hello, sweet dryad. I'm sorry, I was just confused, thinking aloud, my apologies if I offended." Anger pulsed. "Or gods forbid, *bored* you."

Nothing. Perhaps the tree shimmied slightly, a faint giggle hummed, but that might have been the wind. She stroked the tree. "What a fine tree this is." Nothing. No answer.

Meri looked at the sky and saw the aurora had ceased its dance for tonight. Was that why the dryad had disappeared?

The next day, Meri found out exactly why she should have accepted the dryad's offer.

The selkies all gathered, in full armour, weapons shining in the early sun, at the small coastal fairy ring, part of the network of stone circles spread throughout the Callanish landscape. Orla explained, "The small rings have a little power. It will have to be enough. Because we can't be doing with that huge cross in the middle of the Great Stone Circle; the bladderwracked thing crosses out our magic."

"Now, Meri!" said Fionn.

A chill crept over Meri's skin. "Um. Now what, exactly?"

Fionn frowned. "Now, use your kin-magic to open the portal and transport us to the Island of

Orkney, where the puffin-kin told us the magical workhouse hovers between layers of time."

The selkies chorused, "Yes, hurry up, Meri, we want to slash our swords and stab our daggers—" For a good two minutes, they went off into a selkie battle song, all barks and bellows, screams and howls. *"Up in the grey hills, down in the loch! Drink a health to my Bonny Seal Folk."*

It gave Meri time to churn with ideas, rejecting every one. She had no notion what to do. "Ah...how exactly do I use my kin-magic?" she asked, a thread of hope in her voice. They could tell her, and she could just try, and it would all work out, she'd rescue poor Isobel...there. A flicker of something. Like a spark in her mind. A spark that extinguished before Meri could catch it.

"Don't you know?" asked Orla, puzzled. "Isn't your magic natural to you? Wiggle my whiskers, Isobel is your relative, you must be able to call her."

Meri felt like weeping. "I'm old-ish, for a human," she answered. "For decades, I lived a life where magic wasn't real. So I've forgotten what I am, what I might be, and how I might use my talent...I do have *water magic* inside, it grew inside me during my Change, it bubbled up during all that burning and sweating and shivering and ferocious moods. But I can barely control it, only tiny things like making a cup of water swill and spill."

So selkies could frown and glower. A low hum of frustration vibrated in the air: fifteen selkies growling their vexation.

But the relief of speaking, once released, could not now be suppressed. Meri said, wringing her hands, her words tumbling like multi-coloured seaweed in the waves, "I can feel magic glowing inside, burning, yearning; another kind of magic, yes, bigger magic – oh how I wish I will one day transform to a selkie and swim with you all, my dear friends!"

The selkies barked in approval and patted her back with fish-scented hands.

She brushed away hot tears. "But I'm afraid I spent what magic I had in the workplace, on mundane matters. I used my magic to write media releases, and politician's speeches, and helped people write funding applications, day after day, doing little to replenish the source. I worked as a public servant – a civil servant – for more than twenty years. The workplace ate me."

The selkies, for once, went completely silent.

"Oh you poor love," crooned Lenore, a sprightly young selkie, into the stretched hush.

"That is utterly shocking," agreed Ocena. "It's like they took your skin! From when you were a tiny wee cub."

"Yes," Meri's laugh sounded scratchy and full of tears. "Exactly like that." She grimaced. "So I don't know what to do now, or how to do it."

The selkies all murmured between themselves, then a few burst out into a barking, hooting seal song, perhaps an old prophecy, or song about transporting oneself magically.

"Let's just try," suggested Fionn robustly.

Meri took a breath. She'd never actually *seen* Isobel, except in visions. She focussed on that wavering, watery landscape image in her mind. She connected with the blood in her veins, the marrow in her bones, calling, calling her ancestor—

Nothing. Nothing happened. Nothing changed.

Orla said in disgusted tones, "Blast my barnacles, we'll nae catch the rising tide this way."

Meri swallowed, nausea and disappointment swilling in her guts. Her limbs ached, her feet hurt, all her joints pinged with age. She should just go home and read books. Adventuring was for the young.

She hated to concede defeat; she desperately wanted to know that Isobel was safe, before she caught the flight home. And she wanted to spend time with her lovely, funny selkie friends – but surely they'd tire of her, with nothing magical to offer, no capacity to transform.

She said to Orla, as a last, pathetic resort, "Can we get to the magical workhouse another way?"

Orla replied thoughtfully, "Yah, we can just take the ferry."

Meri stared, then erupted in a howl of laughter. "I was so worried I'd failed you all. And we can just *take the ferry*?" She held her hands to her belly as she shook in a paroxysm of hysterical giggling. The selkies, being fun lovers to a seal, all laughed with her, slapping her on the back, raising their arms to the sky and howling, wiping tears of mirth from their eyes. With any other beings, Meri would have suspected satire, but really she thought the selkies just loved any excuse to laugh and party.

Orla added, "Ye know, I believe your years of civil service may yet be a help. After all, if there is any bureaucratic sea-plastic nonsense-rules to deal with—"

"I'll be all over it! Absolutely!" New enthusiasm filled her. She hadn't failed them after all. At that moment, she thought of the dryad. She explained her midnight adventure.

Predictably, the selkies snorted and made dismissive jokes about maudlin maidens and moonshine.

"Let me just go and talk to the tree." Meri walked over to the gnarled pine tree and held her palms to the craggy, fissured trunk, the selkies hooting encouragement in the background. "What of my wish, lovely dryad?" The tree remained a tree: leaves, bark, branches, swaying gently in an invisible breeze. Meri groaned in frustration.

The selkies mumbled and grumbled snarkily about leaf brains and root fungi.

Meri repressed her smile. She almost turned away, then remembered to thank the dryad for speaking with her, and her help so far – was that the merest glimmer of silver sparkle on the edge of the trunk? She paused, breath held: but no. Merely a sunbeam.

Disconsolate, she trudged back to the selkies, who of course had all gone swimming, leaving a great pile of armour and weapons, except for

Fionn standing alone, glancing impatiently at the sparkling sea. "You and I are taking our armour and weapons on the ferry to the Orkneys, while the others swim," explained Fionn. "So excuse, will you? I needs a swim myself before mingling with stinky humans – sparing your presence – on that smelly, noisy ship."

Meri sat on the grassy dune and gazed at the seals leaping and rolling out on the breakers. She almost burst her brains trying to transform into a seal-sister, thinking, *muscle, fur, fins, tail...* A tickle of awareness suddenly trickled down her neck; she whipped around. A bent, aged grandmother stood there unsteadily, smiling gummily.

Meri regarded her with caution. An ancient beggar who would stab her and take her wallet? An old street lady with mental health issues? A witch-crone, a guide on this magical path? She essayed a smile. "May I help you, Auntie?" she asked.

"Hello, dear," the woman said in a thick Scottish accent, with the musical lilt of the Outer Hebrides. "I thought those dreadful selkies would never leave." The air shimmered, and there stood the Uist birch dryad alongside the crone. She shrugged her shoulders in an elegant, ironical gesture. "My friend and I will take you through the portal to Orkney. The magical workhouse is – currently – sited close to the Orkney portal. We will find Isobel, our *meuran-sìthe*, our fairy foxglove, the *sìthiche*."

Meri leaped up and carefully embraced the dryad, who sniffed and made a very haughty, yet secretly pleased, face. Meri said, watching the creature's expression, "The selkies will need to come with us, dryad. I know you don't like them, but they are going to burst in and rescue the *sìthiche.*"

The dryad sniffed. "I promised you a wish. My tree stands."

"What happens if they come and chop it down while we are gone?"

The dryad made a petulant face. "Then I will vanish."

Meri gulped. "So we must save Isobel urgently, for your sake too." She squeezed the dryad's slim shoulder. "The hobgoblin, I mean Donald Mac-Neil, he promised he will watch your tree. He will stop any chain-sawing evil doers."

She hoped.

"Now feel the blood a-leaping, high as the spirits of the old Highland women. Scotland the Brave!" The selkies shouted the old marching tune. Orla split the air with the delicious music of a huge set of Highland bagpipes as they marched through the flat, green Orkney landscape.

"Bagpipes sound a little like whale-song," Meri confided to Fionn.

"Well, yah, that's why we all loves them. Island Scots are part whale and seal from the ancient days. Bagpipes reminds us of our ocean origins."

When there was a pause for breath, the Uist dryad complained, "Why not have a nice orchestra, with keyboards and wind instruments, if you must have rousing battle music?" She stroked her forehead with a languid hand, as though being brave despite her incipient headache. The old one had remained in Lewis in her Scots Pine, exhausted after opening the gate.

The selkies guffawed. "An orchestra?" shouted Lenore incredulously, performing a pirouette. "Instead of stirring marching songs, I suppose you'd love a little tinny flute and pinny piccolo music?"

"Heavenly!" retorted the dryad, her cheeks suffused with faint rose colour.

Meri tried to change the subject. They absolutely couldn't afford to send the dryad off in another huff. She suspected they'd need her before the end, and certainly to transport them all back to their islands. "Do you enjoy stories?" she asked the dryad. "Tales?"

Now the dryad really did look offended. "Tales?" Her voice dripped disdain. She drew herself up. "You assume that because I am fae, I am uncultured?" Her pointed chin elevated. "Naturally I read; Isobel fetches select works for me from the library. Literary fiction only."

"Ooh," riposted Fionn the selkie, a mischievous light in her large brown eyes, her tone becoming plummy and high-pitched. "Lit fic. *A tender exploration of grief and loss.*"

The selkies all roared with laughter. "*A surprising, powerful and emotional novel, full of everyday characters,*" Lenore shouted.

"*Nuanced and truthful,*" sang Ocena.

"A haunting meditation on the complex patterns of familial relations," screamed Fionn. *"A work to read slowly and reread!"* She made vomiting gestures.

The dryad stared at Meri, outrage blazing from her beautiful, heavy-lidded eyes.

Meri swallowed, her throat tightening over the lie she should speak for the sake of peace. This was books, she couldn't do it. "Ah, the selkies do have a point. Lit fic is often very gloomy. Violent. Nasty." She shook her head. "I used to enjoy it, long ago, when I was a girl... but now I think, why add yet more misery to this beautiful world?"

The selkies were still shouting back cover blurbs of literary prize winners, like a mad operatic comedy.

Meri added guiltily, "And I'm afraid these days, I typically find it boring too."

Now the selkies had turned the discussion into a song with a rousing chorus. "Doom and gloom, and boom, boom, boom!" They shouted in unison, Orla accompanying them on the Highland pipes. "Lit fic is not our pick!"

Meri struggled not to burst out laughing, then when Lenore trilled in a high-pitched, long drawn out wail, "*One man's exploraaaation of looone-li-ness,*" her self-control burst and her laughter exploded in great healing gusts of merriment. The selkies crowded around her, laughing too, patting her on the shoulders and back.

The dryad, thank all the ancient goddesses, did not disappear, but patently found some satisfaction in her highbrow superiority, as she merely posed in an "attitude" and muttered, "Philistines, pagans and vulgarians, to a seal." She glanced at Meri, and added loftily, "And to a woman," which pulled another helpless cry-laugh from Meri.

"March on!" shouted Orla, and lit fic was forgotten in refreshing action as the selkies charged, clashing swords and banging shields, towards a steep, gravelly path winding over a craggy, purple hill.

Isobel dripped the tiny splash of water onto the soil.

Day by day, hidden in her attic room, when no prying eyes could report her to the Matron, Isobel coaxed her little tree to grow, to feel its roots in the shallow scrape of soil, to unfurl tiny dark green leaf buds and new branchlets. Day by day, with water and care, Isobel held the tree to the high window so it could get light, gently blew on it, giving it her exhaled breath to make into new leaves.

At first, it strengthened, with brave new shoots and happy aspect; but like Isobel herself, without air and light, nor the natural breezes and far horizons to stare at, lacking the kiss of rain, the little tree began to sicken.

Despair ran riot in her heart. Soon she would have to return the tree to Hiort, the wee Gaelic skivvy, and ask her to smuggle the tree outside again, to save it – and with that action, to lose all chance of escape herself.

But the shallow soil was enough; the bark and leaf buds could do; with that speck of plant life, she could summon enough magic to break her bonds...but that work of magic might kill her friend, this blameless little Scots Pine.

That afternoon, when the Matron came, Isobel stood up from her desk, shoving the chair back and standing tall. "Enough!" she said, head held high and proud, her Island heart pounding brave and strong. "If you want magic from me, I need air, and light, and water, and gardens, forests, wild landscapes, ocean shores. Good food, adequate rest, and for all the old goddesses' sake..." she inhaled a deep, sustaining breath, and shouted, "I need some fucking quiet!"

A wind rose in the room, blowing the imprisoned magic workers' hair back, rustling papers on their desks. Not a strand in Matron's stiff hair-helmet budged so much as a whisker.

The Matron's eyes narrowed. "Are you offering a trade, Isobel MacLeod? You will sign a magic contract to willingly trade your freedom, your talent and magic, exchange ten hours per day, five days per week spent at work, for the rest of your time spent as you wish?" The matron's voice grew smooth. "Outside perhaps, walking along the ocean shore, breathing that sweet sea air you crave? Perhaps enjoying the green forests when you finish work for the week."

"Until when?" Isobel managed to grind out through her tight throat. Right now, she would almost agree to anything, just to get outside *once*; even for the *promise* of getting outside.

"Why dear, until you are no longer needed. Until all your magic has been sucked out, I mean, *redeployed* for the betterment of the world."

CHAPTER NINE
Breaking down doors

Meri called and called to Isobel in her mind. "Hang in there! We are coming. Stay safe, Plant Fae."

Gazing around at the wild weather-battered Orkneys landscape, the selkies marched and sang, throwing out barks and yodels at random.

"Not totally horrible, walking on legs, is it?" said Lenore chattily.

"Yes, this whole marching thing has its merits. So slow, though, where's the speed, where's the joy?" other selkies chimed in. "Yes, slow, getting bored." "Maybe we should transform and swim a bit?" "Ooh yes, how lovely would a swim be right now?"

In fear that the selkies would on mass, toss away their armour and weapons and go for a surf, Meri suggested, immediately wishing she hadn't, "You could try running? Sprinting? Have a race to that twisted tree on top of the hill?"

"A race!"

"Beat you all to that spreading old tree at the summit, next to that fairy ring!"

As one, most of the selkies broke into a run, hallooing and shouting and screaming battle cries or just screaming for fun, charging up to the huge bent tree near the stone circle.

Fearful of being left behind, Meri broke into a jog, surprising herself with how far she could actually sustain a moderate pace, with no alarming twinges, stabbing pains, or indeed, joint failure. She arrived and bent over under the gnarled Sessile Oak, gasping for air and suddenly as elated all her mad selkie friends. They clustered around the tree and the stone circle, laughing, puffing, good-naturally teasing each other.

While the selkies decided to challenge each other to a series of athletic feats involving handstands, tumbles, and yoga twists, Meri examined the tree.

Its trunk was quite thick, twisted with the years of withstanding storms, winds and weather, heavy branches drooping low as though weary, clusters of acorns nestling within lobed green leaves, the topmost branchlets crowned with wreaths of golden mistletoe glowing through the leaves. Meri patted the fissured greyish bark. "I know how you feel. My limbs feel leaden and rather twisted with the years."

She turned to gaze at the selkies' antics, when a sharp prod nearly sent her tumbling in the best selkie style.

She jerked around. A very elderly, imperious woman stared wrathfully at her. "Twisted! Speak for yourself! Charming way to address your Elder. Young saplings, no manners these days."

Meri's first impulse was to step away, yet instead, she held her ground and said humbly, "I beg your pardon, Auntie." Fine, translucent, slightly tattered and worn draperies shrouded the creature's form, with the golden mistletoe looped in a crown over her silvery hair.

The Uist dryad stepped up and the two dryads held a quiet conference, which sounded to Meri like wind in leaves, susurrations, creaks, delicate groans and the faint snap of twigs.

Behind them, the selkies began to sing in an unruly harmony: *"Oh I think I will never seeeee, A poem lovely as a treeeeee."*

Meri snorted back a laugh. Oh they were outrageous! She snapped a minatory frown at Lenore, when the young selkie whispered loudly, "Sap-for-brains. Fungi in their nether regions."

The bent, much-wrinkled Orkney dryad directed an exaggerated scorn-filled tree-face at the young selkie. "Ha! You wouldn't know a leaf nodule from an apical meristem," she creaked at Lenore, who flailed back a step, honking in comical dismay.

Meri bit her lip. Tension simmered. She absolutely would *not* mention stories, tales, books or literary prizes.

In the Orkney stone circle, the ancient Sessile Oak dryad spread her fissured arm-branches wide, and opened a shimmering gateway, a portal to elsewhere.

The selkies, Meri and the dryads stepped through the portal, single file. "Curdle my cockles, here we are!" shouted Orla. The motley rescue crew gazed towards a towering, ancient, top-heavy mansion balancing within a stone-walled garden, lit by mysterious lightning and circled by brooding clouds. "As gloomy and ominous as a prize-win-ning modern novel!" Fionn declared.

Meri laughed, almost dissipating the dread and horrified semi-paralysis that had crept through her muscles. She whipped around, a finger to her lips to gesture for silence. She suspected that attacking with stealth would be completely foreign to her companions, that the notion of sliding and creeping quietly was utterly beyond their power, but the selkies surprised her again.

Orla held up a commanding fist. "Calm now. Hunting mode everyone."

Silently, in her mind, Meri fixed on Isobel and called and called her. "Isobel. *Sìobhrag*. We are come. Don't give up. We are here for you."

Meanwhile, the selkie leader directed a small band to the rear of the edifice, two others to the sides, with most of the selkies, and Meri, and the two dryads who had also stepped from the fairy ring, attacking from the front.

The selkie leader gave the signal, the selkies roared and hollered and screamed like hell itself had opened its gates, and charged forward, weapons and attitudes bristling and ready for action.

They crashed open the ornate iron gates, rushed up the short overgrown driveway, and hammered on the thick, iron-bound front door. They bashed it with mallets and axes – but nothing happened, and nobody came to answer.

"Allow us," said the ancient dryad. "It will be a difficult bit of magic, but there remains water in the cellulose of this wood, who was once, eons ago, a proud Oak." She pointed at Meri. "You! Water Fae—

"Am I? thought Meri.

"Put your leaves, I mean palms, flat on the door, and think of water, only water. Call to the water in the wood, and my tree-sister and me will call to the tree this poor door once was."

There was simply no time to ask the dryad more. Water fae? Maybe it was just a slightly derisory term, like "young sapling" or "branchlet..."

"Focus!" snapped the dryad. "Think of water, of groundwater flowing, of bubbling rivers and streams, of great still lakes and the heaving oceans which feed all the waters of the world."

As the old dryad spoke, pictures formed in Meri's mind, and she relaxed into the spell of water. Running water in the grass, rains pouring down, rivers rising, lovely waterfalls, with spray and water droplets winking rainbows in the sun...fresh watery scents, rain after drought, young leaves swelling...

"That's right," creaked the dryad so softly Meri barely heard her, so immersed was she in her water dreaming...

The ocean lifting her and carrying her, water everywhere, in the ground, flowing in the fungi network in the roots of trees, trees talking to each other through the movement of water, in and out, up and down, sugary sap fizzing in her veins in the springtime...

And the great door swelled, groaned, and burst open, slamming heavy doors to each side.

The selkies charged.

CHAPTER TEN
Whale of a Time

The huge whale rolled in the ocean swell, far out where the great green depths welcomed his bulk, where horizon melded with sea and sky. The mighty thrumming in his blood called; the great seasonal migration the whale pod made every year, as the tides grew cold and he took his pod far from the massive southern ice continent all the way up coastal Australia, basking in the warm, to the islands in the tropics and then all the way back down again.

The migration was as fundamental to him as spouting water from his blow hole, the call, the rhythm—

What was that?

Listening, he rolled around in the ocean swell, the pod slowing around him, mothers gathering their calves, calves nudging their mothers' mammary slits, and the whale mothers squirting the thick, rich, creamy milk into their babies' mouths...

There. A faint song, a whale song, so full of grief and need and desperation...

Surely a trick: another harpoon boat, killing the best of them, the most intelligent, the most daring, the ones who went close to the ships to talk to humnans, and what did they get for their trouble? An ugly, savage death, bleeding on the end of a steel harpoon, hung high from a ship, carved and dismembered for their blubber and baleen.

The whale was too old and wily to be caught in such a way.

The song, there it came again, drifting like plankton, eerie and faint, with more than a thread of magic...a whale song like the old songs he'd sung when he was just a baby humpback whale, of which he still wove threads of melody into the pod's new songs.

Keep swimming. Maybe just a whale from a far land, different.

But all the whales of the oceans of the world, by the end of the season, all sang the same song, originating from the whales of the great southern hemisphere. They were joined in the same song, and now, he should see what the strange whale meant by singing such a different, old melody that he'd believed lost in the mists of time.

"Keep swimming," he told the pod, singing the song for them so they would keep singing it on their great northward migration.

The males and mothers took up the song, and the swimming, and the pod moved off.

There was both safety and danger in whales swimming together; more easily spotted by the harpoon boats, yes, yet also easier to attack, to lift and heave those boats, or for the pod to scatter, to distract the boats while the mothers and calves swam away, away. In the old days, the whales attacked the boats, upending them, smacking them with their tails until they broke; or befriended the humnans, leading them to other prey.

Now, the ships had radar and deadly fast weapons. Staying away from those waters where the ships were known, was the best course. Of course, whale youngsters tried to tease the ships, to taunt them, then outswim them. The whale knew the humnans thought that whales were getting smaller.

Now he rolled for a while in these warmer seas, repressing the call of the migration, the call of duty to his pod; the call tickled in his mind like a barnacle.

Stronger was his duty to a lone whale, a female whale who sang a very old song, laced with magic. The whale knew it could by some dread new device invented by humnans to lure the largest bull whales close, similar to the sirens in Greeceland who teased and tormented sailors to their enslavement.

But he went to find out anyway.

"Now there's no retreating, For the magic clans are waiting, Every heart is beating, For honour and for fame!"

How the mighty doors crash open like a giant drum roll! How we seal-sisters yowls and howls and barks, seal-*bansìthe* coming for you, magical tyrants, growl, growl. Ooh how us blood beats for the glorious battle!

Us friend Merilea's face is terrified but laughing too, bright eyes wide as a seal's, mouth gasping, legs running. I pulls her along, come seal-sister, come lovely, fight, here's a sword, here's a shield.

Ahoy, Guards ahead! *Men* dressed in heavy, magical armour, flashing sparks from weapons, striking lightning at the dryads—

"Form up! Protect the trees," yells Orla, and we shoves Meri and the dryads behind us, so the lightning cannot make fire in their branches.

We selkies surge like ocean waves, like high breakers, tumbling and rolling, handstands and flips, we meets every flash with our shields, laughing and taunting, now us close in, we fight!

Hahah! Hahaha-hahah! With a bark and a honk and a hard slap of our tails, jab the men, slash and smote and break and stun. Falling guards everywhere, onwards selkie-sisters!

"Loud the winds howl, loud the waves roar, thunderclaps rend the air!"

"I know that one!" shouts Meri and she laughs and runs and sings with we.

A heavy thump from a guard landed in Meri's midriff; the knock propelled her through the edge of the wild melee, vision sparking, breath gone. Bang on head, nausea, stars. When she came to, the hallway was deserted, apart from two heaps of groaning guards. By all the hells, here she was alone, with those terrible weaponised magical assassins stirring. She rose dizzily onto her hands and knees, suppressing a loud groan, and crawled quietly to the nearest doorway and pulled herself through. She put her head on her knees and sucked in air, then looked around. Some kind of dark, vacant office. A paid-work memory-chill shivered through her. Her hard-of-hearing ears strained, worried she'd miss a stealthy, sinister tread, or a dark murmur of intent.

Meri flattened herself against a wall of cupboards, her heart thundering loud enough to drown out the sound of marching boots coming nearer. She ducked and slithered behind a desk, hurried around a corner and melted into a dark space. Stay still, that was the secret. Still as the air, silent as the shadow.

A scream split the air. Running feet, wild yells and the terrible clashing of swords and heavy thunks of weapons landing.

Now. Around here, if she knew anything about bureaucracies, the workers would be in the heart of the building, seated away from distracting things like sunny windows with views of freedom... She rose to her feet and crept through the opposite doorway, and down a long, dismal hallway...ah ha!

Stay out of eye level, that was the trick to hiding. She crouched low, pressed herself to the edge of the door, and peered around.

Her stomach churned with bitter fear and disgust. She beheld a whole room of workers, sitting hunch-shouldered at their desks: tall, thin people with greenish skin. Bearded dwarves. Fine-featured folk who looked so elvish even without the giveaway ethereal beauty and slender, pointed ears. Three Blue Men, a troll, a huldra and a huddle of pookas. A faded woman with an echo of a selkie, her spark and sass extinguished. Meri swallowed a pulse of alarm for her valiant allies.

Footsteps, the clanking of armour, the heavy smell of sweaty men bent on fighting wafted into the room. She ducked down and scuttered along a wall. There. Silver curling hair, pointed chin jutting rebelliously. Isobel!

Haphazard plans ran through her mind like cars at a freeway roundabout. This room filled her with a familiar, habitual lethargy. She knew *exactly* how the workers felt, why their bodies had that low-air, tired slump. Chained to desks in an open-plan office. She'd been exhausted by work, hollowed out, drained, even as she'd given endlessly from her talents and strength.

A realisation blistered her brain: a deep part of her had always known she had magic. She'd dispersed that magic, giving it away without care, in the mundane workplace for mundane matters – because, of course, magic didn't exist, right?

Predatory colleagues sensed that hum of silver-gold magic; they circled and closed in, to steal what magic they could, to drain it off her like invisible silver blood, leaving her exhausted and headachy. The remedy was walking in nature, gym classes, yoga; when she was younger, for years she'd got drunk with her friends and danced, dulling the mundane world and its shrieking demands, until she discovered exercise and nature-bathing had exactly the same beneficial effect.

Her superiors demanded more and more work, more and more magic, then claimed the work as their own.

A flare of anger lit inside. Meri was surprised she didn't transform into a beacon, she was so lit with fury. They'd get Isobel out of here. And then, they'd work out how to free them *all*, all the tired wage-slaves, all the exhausted folk wondering what the alternative was to selling your precious days for a paltry few weekend hours of food, privacy and comfort – and that was for the lucky ones.

She scuttled over to the desk next to the woman she believed was Isobel, tugged out a chair and sat. She risked a quick glance at her relative, whose blue eyes widened with absolute terror. Meri put a finger to her lips. Shh.

***

The whale swam closer to the shore, as close as he dared without stranding himself – worried about the risk his pod might follow him and strand too. The song came from land! What fell magic was this? Not wrong like sea temperatures heating and coral bleaching white and dead. No, this felt *good strange*, like a sudden wild storm with gusting rain, like a feast of darting silver fishes.

Then, the old magic, the magic of his line, almost forgotten, never used since he was a tiny calf, fizzed in his body: the booming power of a half-transformation: The Colossus.

Transform.

It had been so long, a whale's lifetime, a generation since he'd transformed to this shape – it was forbidden.

Help us, urged the song in his mind.

Transform.

He meditated deep within himself, willing the change; and when his body transformed, he rose majestically from the sea, water pouring from his colossal form; he ran full pelt on his mighty legs through the churning waves to the land, sprinting hard, following that faint, urgent song.

There! A building, magic sparking from the roof and walls. He battered down the rear barrier and launched himself into scenes of upheaval.

The Colossus charged into the battle with an almighty roar, swatting armoured men like sprats as he waded towards the whale call.

And then it stopped.

"Isobel? Is it you?" Meri whispered. She had only seen the plant *siobhrag* in visions. The ancient, yet unwrinkled face. The bright Viking blue eyes of the Outer Hebrideans.

"Merilea!" gasped her relative, confirming her guess. "No. You mun go, flee, flee now lass, don't let them catch you, this place is *hell*—"

"Not without you," said Meri stubbornly. "Look at you! Skin and bone, drooping with weariness, grey with fatigue, dehydrated..."

Meri became aware that half the room was peering over their desk barriers, others standing and craning their necks. "Back to your work!" she shouted in her best boss impersonation. To her amusement, most of them did. She said to Isobel, "Bit depressing that that worked. Means the folk here are leached of any volition or agency."

"Don't waste your pity. Look – as we speak, two folk are running for matron. *Get ye gone, lass!*"

"The selkies are here," Meri whispered. "And two dryads, one very powerful. Quick, stand up, I'll help you." A rattle of metal; Meri glanced down, and her heart squeezed in her chest. Chains! Isobel *literally* chained to her desk! Her horrified gaze flicked around the office. All the workers were leg-shackled to their desks. "What the fuck is this?" she exploded, outraged, just as a large, angry women marched into the room.

Meri had time to see Isobel duck her head in submission, hissing, "The Matron! Run. Run for your life!"

And then, without anyone even touching her, a hard hand walloped Meri over the side of the head and she collapsed like a poorly balanced pile of office stationery, hitting her hip painfully on the hard edge of Isobel's desk before she landed heavily on the floor. She glared up at her antagonist, rubbing her hip, sucking in air, huffing out fury.

The matron stared down at her, a horribly familiar bully-sneer curling on her lips. "Friend of yours, Isobel MacLeod?" The woman snapped her fingers at two uniformed guards hovering behind her. "Right. Take her for magical testing. If she's got no magic, you know what to do."

Meri's throat tightened. Ice clawed down her spine. The men hauled Meri to her feet and began to drag her from the room, followed by the heavy tread of the Matron.

"Fionnnnnaaaaah!" screamed Meri into the hallway, just before a guard waved his fingers. Try as she might, Meri could not utter another sound. Damn it all, how had she allowed herself to be caught? How could she help Isobel now? The selkies! Were her friends safe, or had she led them into stupid danger too? And the dryads... Oh why, oh why, hadn't she just come by herself when the dryad offered to open the gate?

In her fury and despair, she kicked both guards hard on the shins and knees and listened with some satisfaction as they yelped.

Out of the corner of her eye, she saw a skinny, huge-eyed, filthy child observing from a darkened doorway as they dragged her past.

CHAPTER ELEVEN
Magical media releases and Jubilant chaos

The Matron and her bully-guards dragged Meri down corridors and passageways, stopping before a huge steel door emblazoned with the words, "Ministry of Magical Testing, Assessment, Classification, and Quantification."

"I see you favour the Oxford comma," Meri essayed, mainly to cheer herself up.

The Matron snorted and shoved her hard between the shoulder blades. Meri staggered forward into a small room, the door clanging shut behind her. The space felt like a prison cell: dreary grey walls, everything chained down and cemented into the floor or walls. Hot tears pricked her eyes; guilt rose in a bitter tide. Her happy, care-free selkies! Were they even now enduring who knows what torment? She pictured them chained to desks...

And then reviving hot rage bloomed like a garden of vivid red flowers. No! She'd vowed *never* to succumb to bullies again, mainly through avoidance, but if she couldn't dodge them, she'd meet them face on, *fight,* save her friends and the dryads with her last breath, her final energy.

Filled with new determination, scored with anger, Meri rose and paced around the dismal room.

Then they came for her, and she endured what felt like hours of intrusive magical testing: astrology, tarot, numerology, trying to force her to record her dreams, then a horrible prickly, intrusive mental examination by a magical examiner.

They even fitted her with new hearing aids to replace the ones she'd left back at the Hobgoblin Hotel.

"You could have just asked me!" Meri snapped as she was hauled down yet another long, dismal corridor to a thick door emblazoned with the foreboding title of "Ministry of Magical Messaging (Media Manipulation and Political Posturing)," in bold gold lettering, some of which had flaked off.

"Through here," growled her guard, dragging her through a large open-plan office. "No!" silently screamed Meri. "Not again!"

Out loud, she ranted, "I worked as a spin queen," as they plonked her at a desk. "Written words are my thing. I've specialised in government media and communications for decades!" The click of the leg shackle sounded like her last door to freedom closing. "You could have just asked, "What work are you good at?" She grimaced like a mad gargoyle at her guards.

"Welcome to the Ministry of Magical Messaging," said a resonant male voice.

A resonant, *familiar* male voice. She shut her eyes, inhaled, then snapped around in her hard chair to stare at her interlocuter while he sauntered across the room to face her.

"Murdo MacIver, I should have guessed." She fisted her right hand. "The kind of man who tries to cut down a dryad tree. For shame!"

She rose, her leg shackles rattling in a horrid percussion, and gave him the full glare. She summoned her inner warrior. "Release me this instant. Because I will not, and will never, lend any of my magic for your fell deeds, whatever they may be."

Murdo studied her. Then he smiled. His voice slithered smooth and hypnotic. "Fell deeds? Why my dear, nothing so sinister." His expression hardened, his features growing sharp and hawklike. "There is no *lending*. We merely drain your unused magic to benefit the world."

Meri rattled her chains, chills spider-walking over her skin.

What the absolute fuck?

Oh ah! Guards fleeing, hoo hah! Prod those meaty backsides with our spears, jab jab. Knife in calf, mace in back, dodge and fight, whirl and dance and laugh.

But...Beware! Guards running away. Flee, my seal-sisters – curses, too late. Heavy barred gates clang-clanging shut, slamming down from ceiling at either end of the hallway, boom, boom. Seal-sisters trapped!

We smash and crash our weapons against those barred gates, against the walls, then slump. No ocean, trapped in our woman bodies, no seal skins, magic dwindling.

"All present and healthy? All well?" asks Orla, and we look about at us, and count ourselves, and check gashes and cuts. Ocena pulls out a med kit from her pouch and we dress each other's wounds. Lenore produces tiny bottles of seawater and we splash our faces and hands with healing salty ocean balm.

"All well, Orla," we chorus.

"Time for a song then," says she, so we bark, *"It's some gat swords and some gat nane, And some were dancin' mad their lane, And mony a vow was ta'en!"*

Three guards come to the bars. "Stop that infernal racket," commands the leader.

Lenore trills, *"Come like the devil, Flora Macgillavry; Skelp them and scaud them that proved sae unsisterly!"*

And seal-sisters all shout and sing, banging our weapons against the bars, making a huge joyful ruckus. Lenore invites the guards in for a dance. I swear one laughs.

A new guard comes. He peers in at us, rattling the bars of our corridor cage. "Enjoy your merry party, for now," he jeers, and jabs his spear ineffectually at us through the bars. "You'll be taken for magical testing as soon as reinforcements arrive."

Uh oh. Trouble looming like a hungry shark shadow. Seal-sisters gaze at each other.

Young Lenore drapes her flipper over my shoulders and whispers, "Fionna, my darling, I have the bestest idea! I will bedazzle them with the pretty songs I learned from the sweet siren-folk last winter."

Wenda hears, despite losing hearing in her left ear from explosions set off in commercial fish farming. She nudges close. "Ha! Siren-singing. You'll have these bladderwracked fools of men mooning after us, Lenore. Stalking we, stealing us precious skins, spreading tales of submissive seal-wives across their barnacle-encrusted, man-stinking taverns."

Lenore laughs. "The songs are pretty enough to wake a dryad, I promise. You'll see."

Orla and me grimace at each other. I stroke Lenore's pretty pale hair. "It's so male-gaze to get out of a tight situation using females wiles. We are warriors, my heart. We fight!"

Stomping sounds echo down the hallway. Three more guards arrive. Our first guards, the ones who were almost relaxing and bantering with us straighten up and salute. The nasty guard bangs the bars again with his spear. One shouts, "Move away from the door!" He holds a giant electronic key.

"Sing then," barks Orla softly. "Sing your sea-siren songs, spell them and dizzy them, charm and confuse."

Lenore begins the song and we all pick it up and hum and sing the chorus in multi-part harmony. Together we seal-sisters weave an opera of forbidden desire, of enchantment, of one's heart's impossible yearning almost within reach...if only...

"If only...you unlock the doors," urges Lenore, braiding the melody pattern in soaring sonatas of emotion. "Open the bars, free us, be our champions, our lost heroes risen once more..."

The barred gate rattles open. Quick smart, fast as a dolphin leap, Orla, Ocena, Wenda and me smack the guards hard on their stupid craniums, jab their solar plexuses, take out their knees, trip them and pummel them. Two crawl after Lenore, eyes wild and wild, hands grasping.

"Leave them!" shouts Orla. "Run!"

We run.

Oh no! We turn a corner, backpedal, backing into each other. A large contingent of guards and magical folk with unpleasant expressions march towards we.

Seal-sisters trapped again. We look forward. We look back.

"Shield wall!" yells Orla. Despite our present danger, we laugh – as humans us watched the Gladiator movies a while back.

And for fun, to psyche out our antagonists, we cluster up in military formation.

Just then, a huge cracking, grinding sound rends the air. The walls start to crack.

Meri snorted. Chained to a desk again, and not even metaphorically.

Nah. Nup. Nope. She'd rip this place apart before she surrendered her freedom again.

This worker would continue where she'd left off in her toxic office back at home. Saying what she wanted. Wearing what she liked, no matter how "age inappropriate."

So she stood tall, ignored the rattle of the shackle, and said satirically, "This is more like Ministry of Magical Media Manipulation, if I know anything about modern communications."

The young man, some kind of supervisor, regarded her steadily. Damn. No humour lit his eyes. And sadly, probably not much intelligence. Just a nasty gleam. Meri sighed. Oh well. Welcome to her familiar jungle.

"Your first task for today will be a media release and feature story with the call to action, 'Let's Make Magic Great Again.'"

Meri laughed out loud. Then stopped abruptly. "Oh! Not being funny? For a moment there, I hoped...foolishly, obviously."

The man frowned.

Meri decided she'd had enough of this whipper-snapper's rudeness. She seen his type so many times before she could have made him in ginger-bread. "And your name? Or are you some rando with delusions of grandeur who thinks he can order—"

"Guard!" snapped the man. When two guards arrived and stood threateningly behind him, he reached forward and twisted a pinch of her skin. "You will refer to me as Supervisor Dickon."

"Hey, Dickbrain," said Meri. Muffled snorts sounded near her. "You want me to write media and features, for that matter, policy lines, FAQs, 'if asked' lines? Then I need to align with current policy. "'Lets Make Magic Great Again' is *not* a Call to Action. That's just a vague slogan; I need specifics. What do you want people to actually *do*, believe, repeat? *That* is the Call to Action."

He stepped close, rage contorting his features like a terrifying plastic horror mask. "Just do it," he said.

Meri beamed sunnily. "One of my favourite mantras, for sure. *Just do it.* Just keep doing it. You want me to weave that in?"

Unfortunately, her new foe didn't actually have an apoplexy, though he came within one extra blood surge. "Write the damn media release, *Let's Make Magic Great Again*, and ring the bell when you are finished."

Meri shrugged. *Nice* never got you anywhere with this sort. "In other words, you have no idea? Recent promotion, is it? Out of your skill level, that's if you have one? What were you, a prison guard who manoeuvred and wrangled his way into the office?"

Before he could reply, strike her to the ground or smite her with magic, assuming he had any, Meri yelled to the room, who in the way of offices everywhere, were all listening avidly while pretending total focus on their work, "Anyone?

Do we have lines, policies, content of any kind? Or am I writing it fresh?"

A black-haired man with a lithe vibe shimmied to his feet. "It's the lazy man who laughs last, Supervisssor Dickon."

Meri laughed. She actually laughed in this dreary, terrifying, soul-destroying prison.

Meanwhile her enemy had gone white and then red with fury. "I want that media release," he growled. "Or I'll send you for magical reassessment – perhaps to cleaning duty."

OK, that was a good threat. The man must have some insight. Cleaning corporate office toilets – ew. She shuddered. He stormed off.

Her new friend, Vasuki, emailed her the key messages and lines he had been using. By the time Dickon returned, Meri had created a list of comms resources and documents, plus a draft media release and outline for a feature. It was kind of fun, like exercising under-used limbs, despite the torrid atmosphere and the literal chains.

~OFFICIAL~ MINISTRY OF MAGIC ~OFFICIAL~

10 June

Calling all wizards, witches, banshee and fae! Calling gremlins, gargoyles, goblins and giants.

Unlock your hidden Talents! Let your magic shine. Discover your magic type and find your elite group. Play to your strengths.

Here's how: come into the Ministry of Magic for magical testing. Let us help you discover and im-

prove your magical Talents. Weary of working alone? Hang out with your magical peers and unite with the magical community.

Free for a limited time only: rush in before magical midsummer meadhan an t-samhraidh.

Come on in! It's time for magical folk to rule the known and unknown worlds once again.

Despite Vasuki's apparent helpfulness, Meri hesitated. Should she show her new 'friend'? All kinds of frenemies existed in the civil service, those who pretend friendship and claim your stuff, or stab you in the back to curry favour and leapfrog over you.

What the hell. "Vasuki? What do you think?" For fun, she made it into a paper aeroplane and missiled it across the office to her ally's desk. "Do you think this will pass muster? What will happen to me if Little Dick hates it?"

Vasuki's dark eyes flashed with laughter. "Not to worry," he replied comfortably. "We'll burn that bridge when we come to it."

Meri laughed. Was the man serious? Or deliberately speaking malaphors and malapropisms to make her giggle? Meri felt that pleasant tickle of new friendship, that flash of curiosity about her colleague and attraction to his company.

Supervisor Dickon returned, snatched a copy of the release from her hand, scanned it, and gave an abrupt nod. "Suitable. Now write this one. You've got thirty minutes."

Her mood plummeted as she read the brief. Very sinister. After her years writing political documents, it was scarily easy:

~OFFICIAL~ MINISTRY OF MAGIC ~OFFICIAL~

10 June

Magic is for sharing.

Are your magical elders giving you trouble? Holding fast to their unneeded spells and charms while their younger relatives can barely summon a cantrip?

The Ministry of Magic is calling for you to bring your elders in to donate their excess magic – they often have far more than they need, accumulated over a lifetime.

Magical testing has shown that excess magic causes pain in elders' muscles and joints. Releasing concentrated magical energy will ease their discomfort and distress.

Its time elders shared their hoarded, unused magic with younger folk. That's only fair.

Elders will be treated with warmth, comfort and respect. They'll spend time with other elders in fun social activities. So don't delay, improve the lives of everybody by bringing your elders into the Ministry of Magic.

*All relatives will receive a generous share of drained magic.

At mealtime, they were unshackled and permitted to run, walk and shuffle to the outside. Meri's heart picked up. She wanted to run miles; besides, the call of the sea was there somewhere, insistent, like a low hum pitching higher and pulling strongly.

Meri paced next to Vasuki, noting that the others gave them a wide berth. "What's up with them?" she asked. She summoned some social courage. "Am I toxic trouble to them, so they are avoiding you too? I'm so sorry."

Her friend laughed. "Itssssss me," he said. "Snake man." He regarded Meri. "I won't mind if that ssssscares you."

Meri felt her eyes grow huge, her mind explode with questions.

"Thank you for your help," she said instead. "I wonder...have you heard tell of any...seal people being captured?" She almost added, *they are my friends and I need to get them out,* but she didn't really know yet if this man was friend or foe.

"It's the early seal who catches the worm."

Meri chuckled, grateful for the snake man's charm and fun.

As they were marshalled back to work, Meri resolved to be as over the top as possible, overt in her communications, ostensibly delivering the required wordings yet sending a secret message of extremism to anyone paying attention.

A dark-eyed woman moved through the crowd and bumped Meri's left side as they funnelled toward the corridor. "I'm Jaswinder," she said in a low voice, looking around to check for eavesdroppers. She nodded when Meri said her own name. They stepped forward together, then Jaswinder pulled Meri to the edge of the crowd. "Vasuki has snake magic," she murmured in Meri's ear. "He is a king of the naga, the snake gods, worn by Shiva around his sacred neck, and thus has the divine in him, and is revered by our people. The Ministry is stealing his magic – and draining his divinity."

A guard yelled, pointing a red-lit weapon at them; they hastily stepped back into the flow and merged with their colleagues. Meri glanced askance at Jaswinder, checking for subterfuge; these were symptoms of a toxic workplace, she well knew: hypervigilance; loss of trust; feelings of powerlessness. Jaswinder caught her gaze and showed her a clenched fist, hidden down by her ribs.

As she walked, horror lanced Meri's guts. She felt like she might be sick. This was the worst bullying and theft she had ever experienced. And then a rallying thought steadied her: all her workplace trauma had led to this, and she refused to take it anymore. She had the knowledge, and the tools, and the clear sight.

She met Jaswinder's gaze and clenched her own fist in response.

They smiled. And that shared smile was a promise.

On the second day, she was herded to a new giant open plan office. Meri gazed around, stood up, and dragged her chain and manacle as far as it would reach, (not far), over to the flora fae's desk. Thank goodness.

Isobel stared at her, eyes wide and panicked. "What are you even doing here?" she hissed. "Getting yourself caught too? Now what are we going to do?"

"Why are they draining magic anyway?" Meri whispered back. "What precise evil are they using it for?" She grinned. "Maybe they sell it on the stock exchange?"

Isobel grimaced. "Worse. From what I can glean, they sell it online as a subscription service called 'Daily Magic'."

"A *what?*" A laugh bubble burst from Meri. She and Isobel both checked the room, but their colleagues had eyes down, purportedly deeply absorbed in their work. "Tell me more."

"They advertise it at different subscription levels. For example, magic for projects is Standard subscription. Getting promotions, giving people gift of the gab for those boardroom power struggles is a Premium subscription. Gym workouts and physical vigour will cost you Gold level, and the highest, most desirable is Diamond: Finding Love and being Popular."

Meri gasped. "That is utterly *brilliant* in its evil mastermind-ish way. Monetising our talent and magic!"

Even Isobel laughed, then sobered abruptly and shook her head. "It gets worse. They have specialised products. For example, creatives can 'magic up' their fiction writing or visual art, but the magic is so thin and half-dissolved to make it go further, it kind of works but needs a good deal of the artist's own magic, if they have any at all."

"So they are getting rich from people's deep desires."

"Yes. Millions of people are desperate to be an author. So many books are dashed out with high-priced subscription magic, but because its cut with other things, it doesn't really work."

Meri and Isobel worked in silence for a while, until Meri's questions exploded. "Really, what is the harm in people using a little magic to help them?"

Isobel looked so stern she could have been the quintessential governess. She frowned over her glasses. "The problem with subscription magic is that, as well as being quite inferior, people no longer try to discover their own. As we know, our magic takes a while to discover naturally, and then there's all the training and practicing. People just can't be bothered; or they so totally lack confidence, all burned out of them by this strange social world we live in, that they don't expect to have any magic at all. They've lost hope. The worst people are the ones that snatch any advantage to get rich fast, without any regard for product, or quality, or ethics—"

The sound of the door slamming open cut into Isobel's flow. A high-pitched siren clanged. The whole office covered their ears as they obediently shuffled to their feet.

"We must stop this theft, this exploitation," Meri muttered. "There must be another, fairer way to share magic. Magic schools to help people find their own?"

"Silence!" roared a guard. He prodded the friendly ink monitor squid, Squiddly, with his baton. Meri and Isobel shuffled out with their browbeaten colleagues for their regulation fifteen minutes of sunshine, Meri's mind churning and her stomach knotting. Vasuki was nowhere to be seen. She prayed that her ally was safe, reminding herself that his ability and humour had enabled him to survive thus far.

They put their faces to the sun, starved of air and light. Isobel said, "These last weeks, they didn't let me out at all." Meri rubbed her shoulder.

The child she had seen lurking in the hallway scuttled out and tugged at the fae's hand. "The selkies are captured," she said, and crept away.

Despair cracked through Meri. Her friends! Her beautiful selkie friends! Imprisoned for their Talents, their skins ripped from them, denied the sea unless they gave their magic!

She punched her head and chest, trying to express emotional pain in a physical outlet.

What had she done?

She'd accepted the help of magical beings, charmed by their fun and insouciance, led them into trouble without a thought for their safety, for risk. Meri shook, almost pulverised by her own emotion.

Then she straightened. While she walked, while she could think, she would save them. It was up to her now. No selkie would suffer because of her thoughtlessness, her lack of action. Anger tickled and whispered like a blood tide.

The guards blew whistles. The fifteen minutes of sunshine was over. Everything in Meri rebelled at the thought of returning to that toxic room, filled with artificial light and fake air, redolent with the suffering of her colleagues transmuted into petty jealousies and revenge. Lateral violence it was called, when devoid of all hope, powerless people fought with their own.

The uniformed, full-face-helmeted guards prodded the motley group of workers with batons and spiked maces. As she stumbled, still unaccustomed to a shorter stride caused by actual leg-shackles, something like resolution firmed within her.

No! Her cells shrieked. Office work was so unnatural, completely unaligned with human, mammalian and creaturian biology; sitting there for hours, staring at flickering screens, in the fluorescent light, not using muscles made for movement, nor eyes made to gaze into the distance or up close and wondering; barely using that wonderful, flexible, creative miracle, the mind. Panic welled up like a siren. She flailed her arms, made to turn and flee.

Isobel grabbed her before a guard struck. "Survive," she hissed.

Meri thought about this as they shuffled back to their desks like a dismal footy crowd whose team just got slaughtered. *Survive.* That's all she'd done for all of her adult working life. Survive until five pm. Survive until Friday. Survive until the weekend, the next public holiday, annual leave; relish the few sick days she permitted herself.

What a way to spend this gift of life in human form.

Enough! Fierce, hot, bubbling fury rose within her like a geyser: unstoppable, flaming with molten energy, breaking through rock-hard layers of crystallised emotion.

Meri launched up beside her desk, standing tall and proud. She snapped up her chin, puffed out her sternum and shouted into the void, "I don't know about you mob, but I've had enough!" She picked up a full inkwell and threw it hard across the room to smash against the far wall, splattering black ink like an abstract art prize winner.

"Oh no," someone said, "Not another Australian."

Meri shouted, "I've had enough! Enough bullying! Enough of my own complicity in other people's agendas, enough of subsuming my ideas, my needs, to toxic bosses, useless colleagues promoted through evil nepotism, false ideals, empty promises, materialistic lures, narcissistic politicians." She grabbed all the notebooks from her desk and fired them at walls, at the locked water barrel, at the cupboards and computers and high windows. "I'm sick of all the lies that keep us enslaved, the worst lies being the ones we tell ourselves!"

Tentative cheers rang around the room. A quivering creature turned a vivid shade of lime green and began squealing "Guards! Guards!"

Meri grabbed all the moveable items from Isobel's desk and began hurling those too. The plant fae leaned back, regarding her with a quizzical, amused expression. A huddle of elves sent various stationery items flying like a carousel; the tired selkie straightened her back, regarded Meri with astonishment and gave a tiny cheer. Squiddly the ink monitor giggled, waved all their eight arms and sprayed multi-coloured ink around the room.

Creating chaos was fun! This wasn't so hard! Why had she always been so scared before? The red and black fury fractured old pain and fear deep within her; it cracked through decades of learned obedience. Hot lava exploded all the restrictions, metaphorical corsets, tight bands around her brain, learned repressions which acted like electric shocks if she broke them, all the platitudes she'd chanted to herself.

"I choose freedom!" Meri hollered, hauling up her chain, leaping on her desk and capering. "No more shrinking myself to fit other people, no more restrictions. No more living a mundane life, accepting only what seems safe or easy or possible.

Nah! I'm gonna aim for the stars. Come with me, friends!"

Half the room rose in a wave and proceeded to hurl anything they could grasp, cheering and yelling in excited glee. The other half cowered in huddles, many bleating hysterically for the guards and the matron.

"Let's choose magic," yelled Meri. "Let's choose art, friends, fun, a full, vivid life—"

"And lovely nature!" squeaked a creature poking its head from its mother-of-pearl shell.

"Beautiful, salty, rolling oceans!" called the faded selkie, her large brown eyes brightening by the second.

"Lush green forests and trees, ferns and flowers," sang Isobel.

"And more magic," lilted the elves in silver voices like the lining on clouds.

The room erupted. The magical workforce overturned desks, smashed at their manacles, broke the lock on the water barrel so everyone could drink and the water creatures might wallow in quick showers. They threw everything everywhere, laughing and screaming in a mad, uninhibited, wild frenzy of joy and freedom.

The doors crashed open.

Into the sudden silence, an entire troupe of terrifying guards stepped through and lined up at the edge of the room.

"Join us!" shouted Meri, undaunted, her blood thundering. "Why be an automaton, a faceless guard? Choose your own life! Want to make art?

Grow plants? Dance under the stars? Then throw aside your weapons. Stop being a slave to the evil empire, hollow to the core. Who makes all the money from this theft of people's magic? Not you."

Three guards stepped forward, radiating extreme menace; yet hope surged in Meri's excited brain when at least a third of the security team visibly hesitated, lowering their electric prods and glinting spiky maces. One pushed up his visor to reveal his face.

But not enough of them. The lead guard barked a command. In unison, like a bell of doom, the front row of guards paced forward.

The line of guards parted. Matron stepped through, sneering in vicious triumph. One meaty hand clutched the child Hiort by her reed-like neck. Hiort's narrow frame shivered and shook, her eyes showing white, but her little chin jutted high. Isobel, standing beside Meri, made a strangled sound like a growl.

And then Murdo MacIver paced through like a conquering Roman general, all golden medallions and flaming aura. He flung out his arms and magic sparked from his fingers.

Murdo stretched his arms horizontally, pointing towards Isobel. Horror slammed into Meri like blows while the warlock sucked a thread of golden magic from Isobel toward his summoning palms.

"Don't panic," hissed Isobel, who seemed to be thinning and wilting like a drought-stricken plant before Meri's aghast gaze.

"Stop that thievery this second, Murdo MacIver!" yelled Meri, torn between supporting her dwindling relative and striding over and walloping her erstwhile landlord.

Isobel whispered, "Listen to me! You'll find your strength, your talent, your magic...in calm and...peace." Isobel's body writhed and her face thinned to bones and skin. "Still your breath. Seek deep within, to your core, to your truth, that's where your unique magic hides. Shout that truth out loud! Be...that...truth!"

And Meri?

Meri refused to be afraid. *She was done with bullies.*

She channelled her marvellous friends the selkies' insouciance and squared her shoulders. She stepped in front of Isobel.

The Sessile Oak stood in the garden pretending to be a mere tree, knowing their antagonists would not notice the Tree nor the Forest. Just plants, humm. She'd put her Tree eyes on Merilea when the ocean fae was dragged away for testing. Her Tree vision followed Merilea through capture, the magic trials, and the woman's brave bid for chaos and freedom.

The great Tree's outer bark cracked as she chuckled. While she disapproved of such uncontrolled antics, there was no doubt, the storm made one stronger and the wild winds thickened one's trunk.

The Sessile Oak's Tree eyes watched as the magical workhouse guards arrived in the workroom, and Merilea stood tall and alone against them.

It was time.

The Sessile Oak began to hum. She hummed an ancient song, a song of sun and star, soil and rain, the wheel of time across the eons, of saplings and forests, sea levels rising and oceans falling. She hummed in her roots, vibrating microscopic soil particles and soil-dwelling Tree-friends. She hummed and swished her leaves and creaked her branches and puffed mistletoe pollen to drift like sparkling stardust around the garden.

First one, then two, then five garden trees woke up and hummed the song with her. Still in her Tree form, the Sessile Oak put a heavy tread forward. The Trees took a while; they were not dryad folk, merely ordinary trees; but the ancient Sessile Oak could call them and wake them when there was need.

She sent her Tree eyes to Merilea and creaked her branches. The Trees, the Birch jiggling its catkins, the Malus with giggling pink blossoms, and the Rhus blushing vivid red and orange with excitement, marched the short distance to the magical workhouse.

With great joy, they began to tear down the walls.

Seal-sisters huddle. Trouble to the front, evil to the rear. Stuck in woman form.

Ooh ah! Walls collapsing – torn by dryads! Ha ha! "Hello Oak! Welcome Birch, good morrow Rhus and Crabapple. Hail wise Dryads and Trees. You have our thanks."

Quick, this way, seal-sisters, quick, roll and leap, lovely fresh air, garden smells, rescue.

Bit embarrassing to be saved by Trees, I bark to Orla, and she waves her flippers, grinning hugely. "When the battle is done, we will serve brave Trees rotting fish to nourish their uprooted roots."

Myself, Fionn, I yells, "The more, the merrier, what do you say, Dryads? Let's go find us friends Merilea and Isobel. Set free the Fae!"

"Free the Fae! Onward!" the selkies yell. The Rhus Tree blushes with thrill and the Crabapple sprouts a few shiny crabapples among her blossoms. The Trees' trunk eyes are round and happy, shining out from their bark.

Murdo MacIver pointed a long finger at Meri. "Take that rebel fae to the basement." He grinned sickeningly. "For treatment. This one is a dud. Take her and drain her."

Dud, huh. *Basement.* Like every horror movie and historical fantasy ever. *Drain her.* Meri's fury burned up to incandescent. "Robbing women,

Murdo? If you fail to trick us, then you take by force. That what happened to your wife?"

The mage's smile slipped. His mouth opened, but whatever retort he intended was strangled in his throat as loud booms sounded in the passage. And...singing! Hooray!

"The Return of the Selkies!" hollered Meri, dodging one guard and crawling under a nearby desk to evade another.

"...*Drunken sailor!*" finished the selkies in a rousing chorus, bursting through the door in a flurry of seal-sisters, weapons, and laughter. Murdo MacIvor made to run – and was grabbed by a long mossy branch of the Sessile Oak. She stood towering and majestic, her mistletoe crown glowing gold, dangling the warlock by his britches from a high twig. Murdo swore and screamed and struggled. The guards attempted rescue but were subdued by the thrashing dryads.

Chaos erupted as everyone plunged into battle.

Meri checked Isobel, who stood pale and shaken yet undaunted.

The Trees cracked another wall, which fractured with a noise like cannonfire. Jaswinder, Vasuki and more magical workhouse workers poured in and joined the affray. Vasuki's forehead black pearl gleamed as he swelled, a huge, terrifying multi-headed cobra hood rising from his shoulders. The thousands of cobra heads spat venom at the guards and Ministry attendants, causing muscle paralysis and choking.

The rebels would win! Meri's heart soared in jubilation...until hidden doors burst open all across the room and more uniformed, weaponised guards marched in, surrounding the rebel alliance.

Slowly, the enemy gained the upper hand. A Tree flamed in sudden fire; luckily Squiddly appeared and sprayed flame-dousing ink; the valiant selkies sustained cuts and bruises; across the room, Meri saw Vasuki go down in a burst of magical fire; and then matron arrived holding the child Hiort.

"This child will die!" screamed the matron.

"Wait!" called Isobel. "Take me instead of that child. I come willingly."

"No!" said Meri. She looked around. Should she give up now? Tell the Trees and selkies to leave while they could. Isobel was walking to the matron.

Desperation singed Meri's skin and clanged in her mind. Then Isobel turned and looked at her.

The words were as clear as if her mentor spoke aloud. *Find your truth.*

Time to choose. Time to accept her magic, let it flow, be truly herself.

Meri raised her arms, blocked out the noise and drama around her, and sought inside for her Water. She sank into sense-memory of thundering waterfalls with their charged mists; of rivers sliding and gleaming like silver snakes in the sun; of the great ocean, the power of the sea surging like the unstoppable tides through her veins, and then she felt something coming, something huge—

Half the wall imploded. Furniture went flying. The largest, tallest, most giant man Meri had ever seen exploded into the room.

He must have been ten feet tall, with a good layer of blubber and muscle. Huge thighs, massive arms, an enormous chest—

Meri shrieked, "Behind you!"

Armoured guards poured into the room behind him, wielding nasty long, bloodied spears, ready to harpoon—

The huge man roared. From between his shoulder blades, he spouted a gushing torrent of seawater, full of krill and shells, taking out the enemies' legs, spinning them around as the water gushed, carrying them to smash against walls and furniture. Electrical weapons flared red, then as seawater surged, fizzed, sparked and died. A few guards at the rear simply turned tail and fled.

The Trees anchored themselves with their strong roots, one of them lifting Isobel to sit on a high branch. The selkies whooped in excitement and dived and swam the currents, splashing water in glittering rainbows. Across the room, Jaswinder leaped onto a bench and braced herself against a cupboard, wearing a giant battered yet writhing cobra tangled around her head and neck. Meri gasped and laughed as the cobra winked cheekily at her.

The massive man strode through the water like Neptune himself, humming a song of anger and violence. He picked up guards in each vast hand, cracking their skulls against each other and the walls, and threw them bodily in heaps. In minutes, he'd disposed of a battalion of heavily armed, no doubt magical guards.

Meri should have run. But the seawater swirled around her legs, giving a sense of safety and belonging; more, the eerie song the huge man hummed in a throaty baritone now sounded like deep oceans, and migration, and shoals of krill, and the gentle bath of warm tropical seas—

Meri blinked. *What?*

The man strode over to her, towering over her. He put his enormous hands on his knees and gazed at her. He shook himself, spouted a new tide of water from between his shoulders, then bent and peered at her again.

His voice sounded like the hum of the ocean under the moon, an echo in the deep. A calming, vibrating sound deep in her waters.

If Meri let herself go, let herself be taken by the moment, to stop thinking for once, then she could almost understand him...

He boomed, "You called? You sang a pod song from long ago, a song sung over many times now until it has changed. That song lives in me, Hugo of the deeps. Are you a whale? You appear to be a humnan."

"I sang a whale song?" Meri blinked rapidly trying to process. She stared into a pair of clear, beautiful grey eyes, grey as a storm over the sea... A flash of the whale rescue back in Tasmania. "H-Hugo?" She must be mad.

The whale-man said, "You always had the whale-music inside you, always singing for the ocean, always calling to your whale-kin. I hear its hum even now."

She gasped, torn between exploring more of this delightful story, and the urgent and pressing need of her battle companions. "Hugo, there's no time. My friends, the selkies—" Oh gods, did whales and selkies get on? Or did they eat each other? Why didn't she stay awake through those lovely nature documentaries? She coughed. "Please help. You've come in the nick of time, like a hero of myth and fable." Tears sprouted. "Thank you!"

Hugo stretched out a large ribbed, webbed finger and with surprising gentleness in so large a man, brushed her tear away. "Mmm. Salt," he said as he licked it.

Hugo boomed, "Sing with me, Merilea. This whale song will call to the ocean inside every living thing. We were all of us made in the ocean; we crawled out of the sea millennia ago, yet a tiny part of every creature on this earth still yearns to return to its birthplace and its mother, the great fathomless, endless sea. Sing with me Merilea; seal-sisters, sing with us. Even Trees once knew the song of the sea. Sing."

The Trees, the Selkies, Jaswinder and a bruised Vasuki, Squiddly, Isobel, Hiort and Meri sang the song with Hugo. They sang the sound of the great sea, the call of seabirds, the boom and froth of waves, the surge of tides, the roar and hiss and spit of weather forms, the rich cycle of life.

Orla appeared with a set of bagpipes and blasted out the ocean song, the rich minor keys stirring yearning and memory.

People and magical folk poured into the room, drawn by the song: guards, magical testers, astrologers, tarot readers, spiritualists, supervisors. Their enemies' faces became soft and dazed and hungering; then helmets were yanked off, jackets went flying, boots torn off feet; they discarded their weapons in glittering piles; tore off the rest of their uniforms and underwear.

"Return," the whole room sang in a jangling orchestra of bass, baritone and falsetto, a discordant opera of squeals, grunts and sighs. "Return to our mother, to her waters, to her womb."

The guards, magical testers, astrologers, tarot readers, supervisors, Matron – Meri even caught a glimpse of Murdo's naked, hairy bottom – all clustered, entirely nude, at the doorways and wall openings. Then as Hugo sang them, they ran naked, jiggling, rippling, bouncing, and bopping out of the doorway and down the passage.

Meri and the selkies streamed after them. They watched, astonished, as the entire magical workforce sprinted, hobbled, and limped in a giant naked singing crowd down the road to the beach, hell-bent on throwing themselves into the sea, the origin of all life. Squiddly and the Snake people waved and ran after them.

Meri, Isobel, Hiort, the Trees and the selkies high-fived, laughing, cheering and hugging. Meri hugged the Sessile Oak, eye to eye with its huge, wise trunk eyes.

"Now Meri," sang Hugo in his deep, watery voice, "Find your whale-self and we too will go swimming."

Meri laughed. "That's probably the best offer I've had in years! But – actually..."

"No buts," said Hugo and she caught a twinkle of that whale-rescuing, marine biologist surfer. He *was* the whale-man!

Meri said in a rush like the sea water draining from the magical workhouse, "Hugo, I don't know how." Hot tears of frustration stung her eyes. "How I wish—"

Isobel chimed in. "No wishing, Meri. Just be."

Hugo said softly, "You called me with your whale song. You still sing now, soft and constant, a faint vibration." He regarded her with his intent gaze. "Try now. Breathe. Close your eyes. Allow yourself to surrender to your longing for the sea."

Meri closed her eyes but was prevented from going into an ocean meditation by the ribald whistling and salacious remarks of her friends, the selkies. "Ooh whale woman! Suck and blow!" called Fionn, winking. Lenore hustled into a suggestive pose. "Slurp and spout!" "Breach and bowride that delicious hunk of whale-man," yelled Orla.

"Slap those flippers," added Sessile Oak in a branch-creaky voice.

Meri opened her eyes and laughed.

And just then, such a huge surge of love for her new friends possessed her, a tidal wave of gratitude that she had had this experience in the later years of her life, that life could still turn such marvellous corners; and suddenly that surge became a tidal wave, a tsunami, and the selkies' laughter transformed into gasps, and sensation filled her. Her body swelled, her limbs grew large and muscular, a layer of blubber such as she'd never had in life coated her body. Power and strength and wild gladness plumed within her.

Meri unfurled and stood straight, almost eye to eye with Hugo. "I'm so excited, I think I might blubber!"

"Come wee orca," he said, "and let me show you a whale of a time."

Meri could only nod. She waved to her friends, and she and Hugo pounded to the ocean, to a further spot away from all the possessed magical folk, their strides shaking the earth, leaving dinosaur-like footprints embedded in the earth.

At last, they reached the sea, and waded in in humnan form, until the water was well over their heads, and then, Meri centred into her craving for oceans and seas, and breakers, and her body swelled again, and then she was truly, finally herself: a humpback whale, swimming and rolling and leaping high and ecstatic in a breach with her mystical mate.

Meri absolutely had a whale of a time: swimming, rolling, leaping high out of the ocean, blowing and breaching, and other whale antics. She'd never felt so utterly herself in her entire life.

They swam side by side, scoffing krill, scratch-
ing each other's barnacles, and returned to the
deeps for more whale fun. And then, they had
whale-sex, powerful, muscular, water supported,
and utterly liberating. Merilea laughed and cried.

Later, lying on warm sands on a beautiful, remote
beach, in huge magical humnan form, Hugo said,
"Merilea, my friend, my heart. My pod calls me. I
must go back for the migration. Can you feel the
call?"

Her heart felt overflowing; yet his words felt like
one thousand harpoons had punctured it, ripped
it out and fed it to sister sharks. "Of course," she
said, voice husky. And then, because she was sixty two now, and had vowed to be herself, to be
brave, to take life at a run, since the death of her
husband Hamish, to grab happiness and friends

with both hands, she said, not stuffing about, her throat thick with terror, "Hugo, I love you."

And she put her flippers – hands – over her eyes.

And Hugo said, "Merilea, come with me. Come and whale-swim with our pod, and experience the migration, from Antarctica to the Australian tropics. Sing the songs with your pod."

The need for belonging, arrived sharp and fierce in her chest. The yearning for the ocean, to be whale-form... "Hugo, I cannot. I came to learn my magic from Isobel. She is depending on me. I have only just arrived." She swallowed. "Do you have to go?" she whispered.

"I have to go," said Hugo, and cried several whale tears which might have caused a flood in a less deserted beach.

Meri stood up, still in her huge body, and embraced her friend and soulmate. "I can catch planes to visit tropical seas and go swimming," she said. "I don't need the migration. I'll wave at the whales as they come to harbour, just like I have always done in the winters. Maybe – I'm not sure, what do you think? Do I need you to help me change to whale? If not, when you are near, and I hear you sing, I will change into Merilea-whale and swim a small part of the migration with you and our kin, twice per year. This I promise."

They whale-kissed, which is say, gave each other an almighty embrace that shook the sea grasses and trembled the sands, and rumbled in the sea cliffs. Hugo sang while Meri transformed once more, and they swam slowly together to the beach near the workhouse, bumping flippers.

"You can change your mind," Hugo said in soft, enticing, bass tones which rippled from her toes to her crown.

Her heart felt ripped apart as she struggled with herself. Her voice sounded barely above a whisper. "I'll fly back to Australia twice per year and swim with you in the great Migration: I give you my solemn promise. If something prevents me, then please yes, do come and find me! If you want to. But I think I must learn fae magic from Isobel first. She called me. She needs me."

"I will always want to, Merilea. Miss you already."

And then Meri stood alone on the sea shore, watching as Hugo marched back into the sea, dived, and disappeared beneath the waves. After mere minutes, back out to the horizon, a giant humpback whale breached to the sky, and then he was gone.

Wait, her mind and body called silently, *come back*, but she stood determined. Who knew that finding her magical identity at last, finding a soul mate and her heart's desire, could hurt so much?

Then, feeling cold, small, human and bereft, Meri walked back alone to the workhouse. To my friends, she thought, cheering up somewhat. To the selkies, dryads, Isobel, and her chosen destiny.

CHAPTER TWELVE
Portal to Freedom and farewells

The workers began to trickle back to the workhouse, mazed and confused: an orchestra of elves, the restored, happy selkie, Squiddly, the snake people Vasuki and Jaswinder, two giants, a herd of waterhorses, a huldra and troll hand in hand, four Blue Men from the Minch, a cranky changeling, bogles, brownies, a wulver, pookas, and the child Hiort.

The selkies had found clothes of various sorts and heaped them in on chairs and tables in the half-destroyed workhouse. The magical creatures donned guard uniforms mixed with bright saris and neolithic skins, modern trousers and peculiar dresses. They gulped down fresh water as Meri stood behind a table pouring cup after cup. Squiddly and Jaswinder had raided the kitchens and were ladling lentil and vegetable stew into lines of bowls, which were eagerly snatched up by the former magical workforce. At the door, Vasuki presented each fleeing Folk with handfuls of gold and copper coins in various denominations and currencies.

Hiort ran forward and back, directing running, limping and hobbling gaggles of Folk to the Sessile Oak, who stood proud and majestic, her mistletoe gleaming, periodically opening the Portal and waving the Folk through.

"No sign of Murdo and the Matron," Meri muttered to Fionn in a brief lull. She'd swapped water-pouring duty for clothes sorting with the selkie.

"Orla, Lenore and Ocena are down at the beach calling sea creatures and sea birds and holding the supervisors in the shallows until the magical workforce get a chance to flee."

They both ducked as a loud crash sounded and half a far wall disappeared. The Rhus Tree appeared in the gap, its trunk face grinning hugely, its leaves a vivid vermillion with excitement. "My apologies for the racket," it said in its leaf-rustle voice. A tiny pink-chested bird ran along a fine branch and tweeted merrily. A spider dangling from a silver thread then tugged itself back up to its home in the bark.

Fionn waved a hand. "Carry on, Rhus Tree! Love your work."

The Tree rustled its leaves. "I haven't had so much fun since the Druids danced around my planting," it said and stomped away. More crashes and booms sounded as the Trees continued to dismantle the Workhouse. Meri could see peeps of Isobel and the Uist Dryad holding their arms high and out, lending magic to the Trees.

Orla appeared. "Wiggle your whiskers, hurry everyone! The selkies are tiring. The sea creatures are swimming back to sea and the sea birds are wheeling away. Warlock Murdo and the others are waking out from their daze. They are very powerful. They'll be here any minute."

The entire room screamed and gasped, gulped drinks, grabbed random bundles of clothing and streamed out of the door, running hard or limping for the Sessile Oak.

Meri, Fionn, Orla, Vasuki, Jaswinder and Squiddly shepherded the last of them. "Time to go!" squeaked Squiddly, squirting ink in their incipient panic. "Time for us too. Come, friends."

Meri gulped water, tugged her guard's jacket tighter and followed Fionn out from the almost destroyed magical workhouse.

"Hiort," she said, giving the child a cup of water. "Go and get Sessile Oak. We need her to put the Trees to sleep once more."

Hiort ran. In a few minutes, which Meri spent gazing back along the sea road, her heart in her throat lest Murdo and the matron appear, the Sessile Oak plodded into view. Her wise trunk face beamed at them all.

She swayed in a magical breeze. "Lovely Trees! Go back to the garden. Go back to sleep now. You are trees are once more – but we will never forget what wonders you have wrought this day. I grant you an awakening every Imbolc, every new spring, for your blossoms and birds; and a wakening every Samhain, for your Autumn glory." The Crabapple waved a blossom-covered bough; the Rhus waved all its bright branches, the Birch jiggled its catkins.

"You have our eternal thanks," Isobel said.

"Sleep now, my beloved trees, sleep again," crooned the Uist Dryad in harmony with Sessile

Oak and Isobel, then Sessile Oak led the way, with everyone following, to the Orkney Portal.

For a moment, Meri stopped and looked back at the tumbling edifice. "We haven't destroyed Murdo and the matron," she said to Isobel, despair tickling like an itch. "I suppose they will create a new Magical Workhouse, somewhere else."

Isobel smoothed Meri's hair in a wonderfully soothing gesture. "We've done fine work here, lass. We stopped the evil regime – for now."

"True." Meri found a smile. "So we did!"

Isobel took her hand in her gnarly, ancient one. "Come now, my courageous lass, come back to Uist. You found some magic here, made some good, deep, lasting friends, and discovered anew that the world is indeed a marvellous place, vibrating with miracles and tingling with magic. So now 'tis time to learn and harness that magic, and to align it with the things that most motivate you."

Meri took a deep breath and regarded her mentor. "Let me at it!"

They lined up with the others. Meri hugged Sessile Oak, gazing for the last time into her kind, wise trunk eyes. The Dryad creaked, "Goodbye Merilea, whale maiden, warrior, friend."

"Goodbye, Sessile Oak."

Meri hugged Fionn hard, then Orla, Lenore, Ocena and the other selkies, then Fionn once more. "Hell of an adventure!" she croaked. "Thanks for coming with."

"Any time!" Fionn said cheerily. "We selkies adore frolics and fun." Meri could only nod, her throat suddenly thick with unshed tears. She hugged Fionn hard once more.

"See you back at Isobel's beach," said her friend. The selkies leaped and cartwheeled through the Portal and vanished.

And then Isobel, Meri and the Uist Dryad stepped through the Portal and the world fell apart around them in a blurry kaleidoscope of colour and reformed.

The three of them landed in the Callanish stone circle, balancing on shaky legs. They walked to the nearby bay, where Isobel knocked on the door of a tiny, weatherbeaten cottage door, and arranged a ride to Uist on a small fishing boat with an equally weatherbeaten Gaelic-speaking fisher. At Uist, the fisher summoned her mate in a battered farm truck to transport them the rest of the way.

Rocking in the back of the rattling vehicle, her arm around Isobel while she dozed, Meri was shocked to realise that she'd forgotten to feel old, or anxious, for a very a long time. She couldn't remember the last time she'd spoken to Hamish in her mind.

She imagined how this conversation might have gone:

The sunlight streamed through the kitchen window. Hamish sat in his spot, reading the newspaper. "How was your trip?" Hamish asked, not looking up from his paper.

Meri regarded him. "I met magic selkies, fought a magic battle, transformed into a whale, sang whale songs and promised to swim with a cetacean pod on their migration."

Silence.

"That's good then," Hamish replied. "Glad you had a good time." The newssheet rustled as he turned a page.

"Hamish! What did I just say?"

He repeated it verbatim, then went back to the political and sports pages.

Meri shook her head, in awe at his power to repeat entire sentences with no engagement whatsoever of the brain. "I might have had whale sex while I was a whale."

Her husband of thirty-five years peered at her, frowned, waited politely for her to elaborate, said

"Hmgh," folded the paper and wandered out to tinker with his classic car.

Meri laughed softly. When the Uist dryad gazed at her quizzically, Meri smiled. "I'm just saying goodbye to someone," she murmured. "It's time. He will always be in my heart, but I can let him go now. Rest in peace, beloved husband."

"Oh, husbands," replied the dryad, her tone redolent with scorn.

Finally, they stood together outside Isobel's cottage. The violet gloaming glimmered all around them, gilding everything in mauve-gold.

The Birch dryad hunched her narrow shoulders in a graceful Attitude and assumed a haughty air. "Hoo," she said. "That adventure is what comes of mixing with those terrible selkies." But she winked saucily, gave a silvery giggle, and with a deep sigh of homecoming, stepped into her Tree.

Isobel and Meri regarded each other.

"This might be a little late," said Isobel. "Welcome home to Scotland, Merilea."

They smiled at each other and Isobel opened the door.

CHAPTER THIRTEEN
Leap of Faith

Meri gazed at the pink and green aurora weaving and shimmering over the sea like joyful ideas, like the glad hum of new friendships. She cast a fond glance at the irrepressible Fionn, who was currently turning cartwheels on the sand, in homage to the soft, warm, magical night.

She lowered herself onto the machair-covered dune, a vision exploding in her mind, dazzling as the aurora. Like side by side video shorts, she saw herself here in Scotland: free, growing, laughing, empowered, an aura of glittering magic emanating around her; and next to it, a clip of her back at work, hunched over her desk, a shoulder raised against toxic colleagues, her face drawn with gloom as she tried to repress years of feelings of unworthiness, aloneness, fear, working until the very sap in her marrow was almost sucked dry...

The only question was, *why?* Why had she put up with it for so long? She waved at the cheerful selkie, who was doing star jumps and singing rousing sea shanties, and grinned. Time for Action!

She enjoyed a brief fantasy of returning to work and magicking the hell out of those horrid dullwits. Of smiting them with spells. Cue evil laugh, hahaha!

But Orla, the spotted selkie's voice floated in her mind: "Blast my barnacles, don't give them any more air time; you just give them more power to hurt you. Let them go. Forget them. Leave them in their own squalid, noisome swamp of lies and ambition. That was then, and you are different now. You aren't theirs to torment anymore. Flap my flippers, for sure they'll end by chewing up each other."

With the almost telepathic friendship she shared with Fionn, the selkie plonked herself next to Meri. "Don't even think about going back to that Mundane Workhouse!"

Meri gave a shattered laugh. "I'm nervous about money! Fortnightly pay means independence."

"Oh pooh, money. You humans! Surely you've got something in the bank, and if not, who cares? You can always stay with Isobel and eat fish with us selkie-sisters."

Meri hugged her friend, happy tears pricking. "Well, it's true. I've been saving a little every pay for a long time, my Freedom Fund! Maybe it's time..."

"Too right its time. Hurry up and get yourself sorted." Fionn rose, ran down the dune and did a victory dance by the frothing sea.

Yes. She was a new Merilea MacRury, finally on a life path that made her tingle and grin.

Meri pulled out her phone, opened the notes section, and typed:

~OFFICIAL~ FABULOUS NEW LIFE ~OFFICIAL~

28 June

Resignation of Merilea MacRury.

Keen to actually do some Department Communications work for once? Sick of tormenting talented colleagues?

Well today is your lucky day, because Merilea MacRury is resigning.

Merilea said today that once upon a time, she'd loved working as a communications professional in the Department. Back then, her beloved Communications team were talented, supportive, inspiring and dedicated people, from whom she had learned an immense amount.

"From the first, the Region welcomed me, made me laugh, and proudly shared the best features of their job and their region."

"Regional staff brilliantly supported me in delivering Department messages, stories and events."

When asked why she is leaving, Merilea said, "Department Communications now resembles a torture chamber in a Ministry of Media Manipulation, with everyone chained to their desks and drained of all life force while attempting to meet impossible deadlines imposed by the Directorial team.

Merilea paid a special tribute to the Director and Manager. "In a long life in Departmental Communications, I have never seen their equal in unrelenting, vicious bullying and colleague-blaming."

Merilea thanked the Directorial team for her wonderful new life. "I would not have discovered my Magical New Life without their toxic behaviour, nasty personal 'jokes', and impossible deadlines. Thanks to their unacceptable behaviour, I discovered new talents and brilliant new friends."

She encouraged all her colleagues to seek other workplaces. "Bullying means you lose perspective and totally lose confidence.

"Bullying makes a crack in your psyche and the monsters get in.

"But I want to assure everyone that there is a marvellous world out there, just around the corner. Stand up from your desk, take a look and make that first – terrifying, I know – step. I promise you

will find wonders and friends, and best of all, you will re-find and empower yourself."

Merilea begins her Magical New Life as of today.

Quotes attributable to Department Director [name redacted]:

"Wow that woman was tall."

Quotes attributable to Department Manager [name redacted]:

"Thank goodness we will now be able to recruit someone younger who will fall for our nasty bullying."

Quotes attributable to Department Liaison Michael Smith:

"As per protocol, I will continue to direct media to Merilea in the first instance. I may finally get some

actual work done for a change while the media barrage tries to find her."

CHAPTER FOURTEEN
Fae Training

"So did we completely destroy the Magical Workhouse, do you think?" Merilea asked her mentor, Isobel MacLeod. They sat on the renowned plant fae's porch watching the morningstar glitter in the dawn sky, and sunrise kissing rose-gilt blushes over the dewy landscape. "I fear Murdo and Matron are still about, wreaking horrors. They weren't vanquished. Just beaten for now."

"Sometimes 'for now' is all we have, niece." Isobel poured them both another medicinal cup of warm heathery, honeyish tea, her age-knotted hand still pliable. "Aye, that greedy warlock will nae doubt be back. That Workhouse on Orkney is destroyed, but he'll soon be planning another evil empire."

Meri fixed her gaze on the shimmering sea singing to her from the horizon. "Maybe someone will build a magical workplace to benefit all magic folk, with a benevolent boss, people choosing to work there? Perhaps with a cooperative legal structure."

Isobel laughed. "My tea is verra healing, but yon herbs must be giving you visions. The only way we can prepare for the man's next trick is to be ready. It's time for ye magical training, lass. That's why ye hied from the other side of the world to my island."

Meri snorted. "Lass. I'm sixty-two."

"Oh, aye, ye may be near as ancient as me, and a powerful water mage to boot, but can ye channel and weave your magic yet? Nae. In magical terms, ye are but a wee maid."

It was horribly true. Meri had not been able to repeat her fantastical transformation into a whale-kin after the workhouse battle. Perhaps she needed Hugo—

She shut that thought down like an avalanche over a peat hole, before desire for the man had her up and running for the next plane. She'd made a promise. Instead, she said, "Fae training..." She shot Isobel a nervous glance. "Is it all vegan diets, candles and meditating?"

Isobel cackled and snorted so much that a drop of tea shot from her nose. When she recovered, she replied, "In some fae territories they follow that path. Hah! Nae, love, island Folk imbibe the fleetness and noble strength of the deer, the ripple of the fish, the hope in new eggs, the telepathy of the rabbit. People are made of what we consume. Do you want to be as weak as a blade of grass?"

A tiny frisson of rebellion surprised Meri. "Trees only consume sunshine and water." Perhaps she'd had a weird hope she could exist and grow strong on plant foods only.

"So eat a tree."

Meri laughed. "Fine then."

"But you must kill your own game. Eat or use every part."

Panicked swirled in Meri's belly. "No-ooo, Isobel, I don't think I can kill an animal. It makes me sick. I can't even kill a spider."

Isobel grinned. "I'm verra pleased to hear that. I'm joking. Normally the Folk do nae kill their kin and allies. But you must learn to hunt at the right stage of your training."

"So...what sort of things will I be doing?" For a moment she thought Isobel would not answer. The clouds scattered. Shadows dappled the fae's expression.

Her mentor regarded her. "You can expect to rise with the dawn, learn to open and channel your mind, improve your physical and mental fitness, guide lost travellers, use fungi and plants, master weapons and mind magic. You will pay attention to moods, voices in your head, chance meetings, odd strangers, and messages from birds and insects."

Meri stared, delighted. "Are you teasing again, or is that the real curriculum?"

Isobel pierced her with a glare. "Ye'll have to stay and find out, won't ye, Merilea?" She glanced away, then added softly, "I have found another of ye."

Meri frowned, puzzled. "Another—"

"Another niece. She comes soon."

Another woman joining her fae training? A surge of hot jealousy slammed into Meri like a gut-punch. Envy, fear, anxiety all rushed up like past pain with the bandage ripped off.

"No!" The word was out before she could stop it. She wished she could just suck it back down her throat. Her heart rate picked up as she gazed at Isobel, appalled, shame at her own pique mingling in a bitter soup with her newfound determination to acknowledge her real feelings.

She had assumed she was the *one*, Isobel's magical inheritor, and now she'd be training with – *competing with* – some unknown relative?

If only she hadn't spent so much time playing with the selkies, if only she hadn't waited so long to admit to her own magic, if only—

She struggled to find her better self, her true self, the one she was working hard to manifest. "Oh!" she said. She summoned her inner courage and hope, so strong and fierce now after her magical adventures. "That's great for you Isobel, to have two trainees." The words sounded squeezed and croaky, but she'd managed to speak them. Because they were true too. "I'm so excited about the future."

Isobel's Viking blue eyes met her gaze, clearly seeing all that Meri fought to contain.

She gave a short nod. And smiled.

Meri stared at her mentor, shock rippling on her skin. Had she just passed her first fae trial? Sudden happiness bubbled up, fizzing and soaring.

Isobel and Meri clinked teacups and grinned at each other as the landscape lit up with the new day: rose, gold, amber, vivid orange, transformed into poetry and enchantments.

Coming soon:

Fairy Blood Book 2 - *Triumph of the Swamp Hen.*

Meet the Swamp Hen and read about Merilea MacRury's continuing magical adventures.

About the Author

Ava Le Fey adores writing quirky fantasy filled with humour and adventure. She loves the outdoors, and her stories illume the wild landscapes which set her imagination soaring.

Australian Ava has Highland and Outer Hebrides Scots heritage. She often thinks she is part selkie too.

Connect with the Author

Visit Ava at

www.avalefey.com

www.facebook.com/AvaLeFeyAuthor

Email: ava@avalefey.com